Barrett's Law

SARAH RICHMOND

Dedication

This book is dedicated to Avery Allen

Acknowledgements

Just outside Fallon, Nevada on Route 50 on the way to Carson City, stands a Nevada Historical Marker for Ragtown. It is all that remains of the once thriving town. The people who lived there were as diverse as the American landscape. They are now part of American history. My hope is they will be remembered for their hard work, physical and moral courage and family loyalty. Together, they built a nation.

Many thanks to the Fallon, Nevada Tourism Office for their help and interest in this project. Also to the Mark Twain Bookstore in Virginia City, Nevada for their suggestions. For more information about the State of Nevada and the interesting places to see there, please try **www.travelnevada.com**.

Barrett's Law

NEVADA TERRITORY 1861

Chapter One

NICOLENA CARLSON, LENA to her friends, was shocked into silence, a rare calamity for her.

Sitting across from her at his oversized mahogany desk was Mr. Kemp, the owner of the Ragtown Bank and one of the wealthiest men in the territory.

Mr. Kemp had just asked her to be his wife.

"Mrs. Carlson," Mr. Kemp said agreeably as he folded his hands on top of the desk.

His fingers were pink and fleshy, his fingernails immaculately clean.

Lena looked at him expectantly.

"I want you to think of my offer as an opportunity. The territory is growing with the Comstock playing out in Virginia City and many a traveler passing through our community. The Carlson Mercantile will prosper with a man's firm guidance. I intend to open a second store in Virginia City, maybe even in Carson."

Lena found the desk to be imposing and the man behind it pompous, but Mr. Kemp was a powerful man and to contradict him would've been unthinkable in the old world.

"Don't you want to be rich?" he asked.

Finding her voice at last, Lena spoke. "Never did I think about such things. Always, I knew this new country was a place of opportunity but never did I consider it possible for me to be a wealthy woman."

Mr. Kemp licked his thick lips. "You'll have everything a woman wants, the biggest house Ragtown has ever seen, expensive clothes all the way from Paris, France and the respect of every citizen in the territory."

"Instead of marrying me, why not open your own store?" she asked. "Soon there will be enough business for two dry goods stores in this town."

Mr. Kemp grabbed the lapels of his tailored suit and stuck out his chest. "I intend to run for governor when Nevada becomes a state. It's only a matter of time, Mrs. Carlson, only a matter of time. A wife would be an asset to a man with my ambition."

Lena smiled feebly. She could do a lot worse than Mr. Kemp at the bank. He was clean and had the manners of a gentleman. A prudent woman would seize this chance to secure her future.

"Yes, I suppose that's a fine ambition," she said, "and one that any woman would be proud to have in a husband."

"Good. We are in agreement," he said. "I'll make the arrangements."

"Except I need some time to think about your offer," she replied, smiling agreeably.

It was always wise not to let a man take you for granted, she'd discovered.

Mr. Kemp exhaled audibly. "I realize women have a difficult time making up their minds. Consider carefully,

Mrs. Carlson. You don't have many choices left at your age."

Lena bristled. A lady didn't like to be reminded of her advancing years.

Mr. Kemp raised his bulk out of the chair, straightened his jacket and brushed a piece of lint from his silk cravat.

Lena stood, understanding she was being dismissed. Frankly, she needed some air.

"I'm not trying to put pressure on you but my advice to you is to accept my proposal," he said firmly. "I will take good care of you," he added as an afterthought.

"I can take care of myself," Lena replied, chafing at his arrogance. She harbored no illusions that he cared for her. He wanted her dry goods store and the respectability of a wife—two things she could give him.

"Oh, come now, Mrs. Carlson," and here he hesitated, no doubt trying to find the right words to placate her. "All women ought to be under the protection of a husband."

"Not all women find a man's protection worth the effort."

Mr. Kemp puffed up like a rooster. "I'd hoped you'd understand the advantages the marriage would have for you," he said, his tone sharp and condescending.

He'd thought his offer was generous, Lena mused. He saw her reluctance to accept on the spot unreasonable.

"The advantages cut both ways," she retorted.

"Which, you must agree, in a business transaction is as it should be?" He'd overplayed his hand but there was no turning back.

"I will consider the offer," she replied, "and give you an answer by the close of business on Friday."

"I shall be expecting it." With a cursory nod and opening the door, Mr. Kemp released her from the interview.

Lena stood on the boardwalk in front of the bank and drew her red wool shawl closer around her shoulders. It was a splendid morning with the chill of fall weather in the air.

The main street throbbed with activity. The year was 1861 and the territory was changing. The discovery of silver at the Comstock had brought riches beyond anybody's dreams when Ragtown had become a station for the Overland Stage.

This hardscrabble town was home and she was proud to live here.

There was talk that the United States government intended to give out free land. If that happened, more families would come out west. Ragtown would prosper and the Mercantile along with it.

When she and Mr. Carlson arrived in Ragtown, Mr. Carlson used her modest dowry and his savings to purchase the store from the Miller family who'd moved north to the Comstock.

Mr. Carlson had a head for numbers and Lena had worked by his side as a wife is expected to do. Even though they hadn't been blessed by children, her life had been satisfactory.

Her husband had worked himself into an early grave.

After Mr. Carlson had died, she'd considered going back to Chicago where other people from the old country had settled. War raged back in the States and brother killed brother.

Ragtown seemed like a safe haven from the conflict and strife and she had stayed. She'd managed the best way she knew how, working long hours and saving every copper penny. The store did well and Lena liked to think the Carlson Mercantile had become the social center of town.

Still, she was nearing middle-aged and feeling her years. Her body had thickened and her hair had begun to turn silver. Mr. Kemp's tactless remark reminded her of what she'd tried to ignore.

She didn't hold a grudge against Mr. Kemp. The man was a sound businessman, a quality she'd never faulted in a man. Except beneath his veneer of civility bubbled greed. She couldn't abide someone taking more than his due.

Lena did have her future to consider and a wise woman always planned ahead. So she would accept Mr. Kemp's proposal. Her future would be settled.

Lena stepped off the boardwalk into the dusty street. She wanted to enjoy her freedom from the banker's materialistic nature a while longer.

Friday would be here soon enough.

LENA WAITED WITH patience as Grandma Elias selected yard goods from the colorful bolts of gingham and calico. The woman's eyesight was beginning to fail her and she insisted on a close examination of the many fabrics Lena had in stock. The pile of bolts grew too tall and Lena started a new pile.

"What's got you all distracted?" Grandma Elias asked. The old lady hadn't missed Lena's frequent glances out the window.

Lena returned her attention with an affectionate smile. "Just watching a stranger passing through."

Grandma squinted her eyes. "You mean the man on that black mule?"

"Yes," Lena replied. "Do you know who he is?"

"Can't say that I do."

The two women peered out the window, their heads together in a conspiratorial fashion.

The stranger wore a buckskin jacket and wool work pants. His short-brimmed hat was pulled down. He got down off the mule and led the critter over to the watering trough. The man walked stiffly as if he'd come a long distance.

"Looks like one of them placer miners to me," Grandma said. Lena had to agree. Whoever this was had the look of a man used to hard living.

They turned away from the window. It wasn't unusual to have a stranger passing through town. Most were law-abiding. This stranger didn't carry a weapon and looked harmless enough.

Ragtown didn't have a sheriff—a deficiency that Lena was quick to point out to all who'd listen—and it was up to the citizens to keep the peace.

Lena measured out the dark blue calico that Grandma Elias found to her liking and ripped two yards off the bolt. She folded the material and wrapped it in brown paper.

"Getting cold," Grandma Elias said.

"Time to put on an extra petticoat," Lena replied as she secured the parcel with string.

"Don't you stay a widow for too long," Grandma said, crackling like a warm fire. "I've buried three husbands. There's nothing like a man in your bed to keep you toasty at night."

Lena didn't pale with embarrassment, as she would have back in the old country. She'd heard the sentiment many times since Mr. Carlson had passed to his reward. Her husband hadn't been an affectionate man and believed cuddling under blankets a romantic notion of silly females.

She smiled indulgently at Grandma Elias.

The bell on the front door jangled and Lena and Grandma Elias turned to look.

The man in the buckskin coat stood in the doorway. There was six feet of him with broad shoulders that made the doorway look small.

"Good morning," Lena said.

"Ma'am," the stranger responded.

"Come out of the cold."

"Obliged." He stepped inside, closing the door behind him.

"Who might you be?" Grandma asked, giving the man a closer examination.

The stranger didn't seem to mind Grandma's poor manners. "I'm Henry Barrett, ma'am." He removed his battered hat and held it to his chest.

Lena's pulse quickened. Henry Barrett was a handsome man. His eyes were the deep blue of a summer storm in a face that was weathered and scarred. His thick mustache showed a slight sprinkling of gray. His dark beard claimed the lower half of his face and needed trimming. He was a man, to Lena's way of thinking, who needed looking after.

"You're not from around here, are you?" Grandma asked, petulantly. Grandma had her dander up. She didn't like strangers.

"No, ma'am, I'm not."

"I hope you're not a gunfighter," Grandma continued. "This here's a peaceful town."

Mr. Barrett unbuttoned his coat and showed them he wasn't carrying a sidearm.

Grandma nodded, satisfied. "I suppose you're one of those who are mining a claim."

"Yes, ma'am."

He was as they'd guessed, Lena realized, a miner, one of many who'd come to the territory to make their fortune.

"And not too successful a claim by the look of you."

"This is Mrs. Elias," Lena interrupted. "Folks around Ragtown call her Grandma." Mr. Barrett smiled. If Grandma offended him, he didn't let on.

"My name is Nicolena Carlson. Please call me Lena."

"Ma'am," he said to them both and tipped his hat.

Lena would've liked to ask him a few questions but his gaze was on the shelf behind her. She handed Grandma Elias her package. "You'd better go get started on that new dress."

Grandma tucked her purchase under her arm. "I expect I'd better. Just put that on my account." Giving Henry Barrett one last look of disapproval, she headed for the door.

He opened the door for her and she swept past him with her head held high.

"You know how to handle feisty old ladies," Lena said when Grandma was out of earshot.

"She was naturally curious," he said, closing the door.

"What can I get you?" she asked, liking his forbearing ways.

He pointed to one of the jars on the shelf. "How about some of that penny candy?"

Lena blinked back surprise. "You don't strike me as the type to have a sweet tooth."

"The candy's not for me."

"A lady?" she asked.

"You might say so."

"Are you sure she wouldn't rather have some nice toilet water?" Lena reached under the counter and found a blue bottle.

His eyes narrowed.

"This is our best seller," she said, setting the bottle on the counter. The scent of violets was very strong.

He studied the bottle. "How much?"

"One dollar," she replied. "Would you like to take a whiff?"

"No need. The candy will do," he said with a throaty growl.

Lena nodded and looked behind her. "I've got lemon drops, peppermint lozenges, striped candy sticks, licorice and gumdrops."

"I'll take a quarter pound of those lemon drops."

She took down a large glass jar. Most miners passing through weren't given to conversation and Henry Barrett was no exception. She supposed living like he did had hardened him to idle chatter and put him off his sociabilities. Except he'd been as polite as a schoolboy with Grandma Elias, so he'd learned some manners along the way.

His gaze traveled to the rack of new rifles on the far wall. He walked over to them and took down a newly arrived Sharps rifle that breech loaded, saving time and lives. He tested the sight.

"The best weapon sold," she said as she measured out the penny candy on the scale.

"You'll get no argument from me about that," he told her. He stroked the long barrel, admiring the craftsmanship of the stock.

"Just came in all the way from Hartford, Connecticut."

"How much does one of these rifles sell for?" he asked.

"Forty dollars."

Henry opened the breech. "That's mighty steep."

"It's a good price," she answered.

He pinned her with a steely gaze. Unbidden, her heart fluttered like a girl's. He closed the breech with a snap and returned the rifle to its place.

She recognized the problem. Henry Barrett didn't have any money. Like most miners, the lack of ready cash was only temporary. The hills around them abounded in gold and silver for the taking.

"I'll start an account for you. You can pay me when your claim pays off."

Henry Barrett shook his head. "I'm much obliged but I don't want any credit."

"Everybody in town has an account here. It's the easiest way to buy the things you need."

"Thank you but I pay cash or I go without."

She closed the bag. "Very well. Will that be all?"

He took a leather pouch out of his pocket. His hands were worn and rough, a working man's hands. A deep bruise fanned out across his knuckles. He shook out the contents of the pouch and laid some copper coins on the counter.

"What brings you to Ragtown?" she asked, picking up the old coins.

"I'm meeting my daughter."

Lena was delighted to hear he had a family. "How wonderful you have a daughter. Has it been a long time since you've seen her?"

"Better part of a decade."

Lena rang up the sale and put the coins in her cash register. "The candy is for her?"

"Yes, ma'am."

She smiled. He'd spent what little money he had on a gift for his girl. He was a good man.

"She'll be excited to be here with her papa," Lena said.

"I hope you have a wonderful visit."

As sudden as a fall storm, his gaze darkened. "She's not staying. The truth of the matter is I intend to send her back to her kin back East where she belongs."

"But Mr. Barrett, she's traveled a distance for a reunion."

He scowled. "I don't want her here."

Lena recoiled at his reply. She couldn't imagine him turning away a daughter. She saw by his manner that she wouldn't be able to convince him otherwise.

Never had she met a more obstinate man.

She handed him the bag of lemon drops. She tried not to show her disappointment in his attitude. This was none of her affair.

He took the bag and stuffed it inside his jacket. Laying two fingers on the brim of his hat, he said thanks and departed.

Chapter Two

L ENA CHECKED HER watch pinned to her blouse. The stage was due any minute.

Henry Barrett hadn't said what put him off letting his girl stay in the territory. She supposed a man like him didn't feel equipped to take care of a daughter. Placer mining was a difficult life and not one suited to raising a family.

Except she felt strongly the visit should be a special one. A girl needs her papa. Somebody had to tell Mr. Barrett before he made a terrible mistake.

Lena pulled off her apron and tossed it onto a barrel of pickles. She put on her bonnet, tying it with haste. She turned over the Closed sign and locked the front door of her store. The rest of the day would be busy with locals coming in for supplies but she needed to reach Mr. Barrett and convince him to reconsider his decision to send his girl home.

A crowd had gathered on the boardwalk in front of the freight office as it always did. Even Mr. Kemp stood waiting, his hands holding the wide lapels of his expensive suit as he conversed with a group of men. She recognized Big Jim Cole, a rancher running a thousand head of cattle out at the Rocking J, Mr. Woodruff who wrote for the *Territorial Enterprise*, Mr. Belknap the barber in his white apron and Mr. Andresen, who'd just built a two story hotel that dwarfed the other buildings in town.

They'd all been helpful with advice on how to run the Mercantile since Mr. Carlson had died. She was grateful. She'd a lot to learn about keeping accounts and managing inventory, for Mr. Carlson hadn't found it necessary to teach her.

She said good morning to the men and they touched their hats in greeting. Mr. Kemp acknowledged her with a nod and then turned back to converse with the group.

The stage's arrival was always waited on with eager anticipation. The mail bag held letters from family and friends in the States. Before they relied on the stage, the Pony Express came through for a short time but the Express rider had been limited in what he could carry and the operation had lost money. Now the stage brought the mail, packages and passengers.

One day the railroad would cross the Great Plains and connect both coasts. Some doubted tracks would be laid this far south but Lena believed the strike at the Comstock would change those railroad men's minds. The silver ore needed shipping and taking the ore out in freight wagons was slow work.

She heard shouting and the jingle of harnesses. The Overland Stage, pulled by six horses, rumbled passed the Carlson Mercantile and up the main street.

She searched the crowd to find Henry Barrett and saw him leaning against the rough-sawn wood of a hitching post across the street. He chewed on a stalk of dried-up grass.

Lena kept safe on her side of the road as the driver pulled hard on the reins, cursing at the team. The stage came to a jolting stop. The horses were lathered up and wild-eyed with excitement.

Henry came to attention, threw away the stalk of grass and stepped off the boardwalk. He grabbed the bridle of the lead horse and held on as the gelding tried to yank free, calming him with gentle words and a firm hand. With Henry's help, the stage agent released the worn-out team from their harnesses and led them away to the smithy's corral.

A deputy sheriff rode shotgun this morning. That meant payroll was traveling on the stage for the boys at the Rocking J. Except the deputy was slumped forward in his seat, clutching his side.

"What's wrong?" Lena asked.

"Looks like trouble," Big Jim told her. A murmur of concerned voices added to her apprehension.

The driver wrapped his reins around the brake. The crowd started shouting questions.

"We were rounding the bend at Dead Man's Creek," the driver said gravely. "A gang of desperados came out of nowhere and dry-gulched us before we knew what happened. The deputy pulled off a couple of shots. I couldn't tell you if he hit any one of them but they returned fire and all hell broke loose."

The driver helped the deputy from his seat. Several men reached up to ease him to the ground.

The deputy's face was the color of bleached muslin. His eyes were heavy-lidded. His gray flannel shirt was soaked in blood and Lena feared he'd lost more than a man could recover from.

"Belly shot from the looks of him," Big Jim said.

"Let's take him over to Doc McKinnon's place," Mr. Belknap said. He gave the deputy a shoulder to lean on.

"Is the payroll gone?" Big Jim asked.

"Yes, sir," the driver replied and he jumped down to

the ground. "The cash box was what those no-accounts were after."

Mr. Andresen looked down his glasses. "Didn't I tell you? The route between here and Carson City isn't safe."

"This lawlessness has gotten out of hand," Mr. Belknap agreed. "We need to do something about these gangs roaming the territory."

No one in the crowd disagreed about their need for more security but there were more important considerations at the moment.

Three men picked up the deputy and carried him down the middle of the street to Dr. McKinnon's office.

Henry wiped his hands on his pants and opened the door to the stagecoach. Lena could see from her vantage point on the boardwalk that the inside was empty.

"Where are your passengers?" Henry asked the driver.

"One passenger. She couldn't've been more than seventeen. Said she hailed from St. Jo."

"Where is she now?" Henry growled.

"They took her along with the money." The driver looked plenty sorry.

Lena sympathized.

Henry stepped closer to him. His eyes narrowed into slits and his upper lip curled into a snarl.

"How many?" he asked.

"Five of them outfitted in dusters," the driver said nervously. "I didn't see their faces a'tall. They wore flour sacks over their heads with holes poked through. Only their eyes showed."

"Did you recognize their horses?" Lena asked, trying to be helpful.

"No, ma'am. Reckon those outlaws were from around here."

Henry blocked the stagecoach driver's retreat. "Which way did they go?"

"I can't say," the man replied.

With lightning speed, Henry grabbed the driver by the shirt. "How could you've missed that important detail?"

Lena rushed to the driver's side. She put her hand on Henry's arm. "Don't blame him," she said. "He would've been taking care of the deputy."

Henry's face reddened but he stepped aside to let the poor man go. The stagecoach driver pulled out his handkerchief and wiped his face.

The rest of the crowd stood open-mouthed at the sudden confrontation.

"Take your time and think," Lena said, encouragingly. "The gang took the girl and then what happened?"

The driver looked at Lena with gratitude. "Seems to me they headed to the west, back toward Carson City."

Lena despaired. A man could easily hide anywhere in the territory but the gang would have no trouble disappearing once they reached the foothills of the Sierra Nevada mountains.

Henry turned away and walked across the street. Lena didn't blame him for his outburst. His temper had flared but a man would be protective of his kin. Her heart ached for him and his daughter.

Henry headed for his mule, walking with long strides. Lena scurried to catch up with him.

"Where are you going? What are you going to do?" she asked even though she knew the answer.

"I'm going after those varmits." He reached the mule who ignored him.

She touched him again on the sleeve. He looked at her this time with a coldness in his eyes that frightened her.

"What can one man do against five desperate men?" she asked.

"I can't tell you. All I know is that my girl is a hostage and I mean to rescue her."

"You can't go out there alone. Why don't you wait for Big Jim Cole and the others to ride with you?"

"I don't need their help," he said.

"The gang is moving to the west, if the driver has remembered correctly. Let the sheriff in Carson City take care of them."

"If that's where the gang is headed. Those men have a lot of places to hole up in between Deadman's Creek and Carson. My daughter don't have much time to wait on a posse."

Lena knew he was right. A city-bred girl would have a difficult time out here in this restless land. She refused to think about what might happen to Henry's daughter in the company of five men who scorned all that was descent and good.

He turned his back and adjusted the cinch on his saddle. He'd nothing more to say, his mind made up. Unhappily, her powers of persuasion had met a wall of granite.

Lena hurried back to the store. She couldn't let him leave town unarmed. She was standing on the boardwalk as he rode by.

"You'll need these," she said, holding out the new Sharps rifle and a box of cartridges.

Henry reined in his mule. He eyed the weapon with a man's natural longing.

"There's five of them, Henry and you'll need this breech loader to have any chance."

"No, thank you, Ma'am."

"You need these, so quit being such a stubborn old goat."

Henry Barrett pushed his hat back on his head. The remark brought a wry smile to his face. She hadn't meant to speak so harshly but she didn't want his pride to be his undoing.

He took the gun and ammo from her.

"I'm much obliged. I'll pay you back as soon as I return." He opened the box and put a handful of ammo in his coat pocket. He tucked the box inside his saddlebag and laid the gun across the saddle in front of him.

"Just bring that girl back safe," Lena said.

Henry touched the brim of his hat. "That's exactly what I intend to do."

Lena wrung her hands as she watched Henry riding out of town.

For heaven's sake, don't get yourself killed.

With a kick to the ribs, Henry urged his mule to get going.

Five men on horses would be easy to follow, Lena reckoned, as long as they stayed on the road, although the gang did have considerable lead time. And they were riding horses which were faster than an old black mule.

If they headed into the hills, Henry's sure-footed beast would make good time in the rock-strewn trails compared to horses. One of their mounts carried two riders, slowing them down.

She looked up at the sky. Heavy clouds gathered in the east. By nightfall, they'd bring thunder and lightening and welcome rain. No time to be outside, Lena thought. With the weather changing and with that mule, Henry'd be lucky to cover the ground to Deadman's Creek by dusk. The gang would have to find shelter for the night. Henry

Barrett would do the same.

She said a prayer, even though a girl of eighteen and an irate papa against five brutal men bent on mayhem were poor odds no matter how you sliced it.

LENA HEADED FOR Dr. McKinnon's place at the other end of town. A crowd of concerned citizens milled around the doctor's front door waiting on word about the deputy's condition. She pushed her way to the front. Everybody discussed what might be done about the gang. Their voices grew louder as opinions were expressed and rejected.

Mary McKinnon met Lena at the door. They'd become fast friends when Lena arrived in the territory. Their friendship had strengthened after Mr. Carlson died. Mary hated living in Ragtown but had given up urging her husband to take up his practice in a more civilized place. Dr. McKinnon's dedication to the small town had won him the respect and love of all of the residents.

Mary fidgeted with a broach at her neck. "Lena, thank goodness you're here." She beckoned Lena inside the log cabin that served as a home and office for the town's only doctor.

Lena hurried inside. Mary had set out breakfast with her best china teacups and saucers. The doctor's fried eggs and cornbread sat half-eaten on his plate.

"I came as soon as I could. Is there anything the doctor needs from the mercantile?"

Lena peered into the next room and saw Dr. McKinnon put a handful of instruments into a pan of water.

"You'd better ask him." Mary retreated to the kitchen for more hot water.

The deputy lay on a table. His eyes were half open, his jaw slack. His shirt lay crumpled next to him, covered with blood. His midsection was wrapped with gauze, a bloody stain already showing through.

The smell was distinctive, of carbolic and blood, a smell never forgotten. She feared the boy was gone but then he groaned.

"Is there anything I can do?" Lena asked. "Anything I can bring from the mercantile?"

Dr. McKinnon wiped his glasses on a white handkerchief. Dark spots stained his wool vest. "Thank you, Lena. I've got all I need for now. This boy's lost a lot of blood. We'll have to wait and see if he pulls through."

The deputy raised a weak hand to his mouth. She looked at the doctor. Dr. McKinnon nodded.

Lena poured a glass of water from a jug. She helped the deputy sit up. He was very young. His shoulders were thin and his bare chest had spouted only a fistful of soft hair.

She held the glass to his lips. With a great deal of effort, he tried to swallow but started coughing instead.

Lena patted his back until he quieted. The effort had cost him what strength he'd had left. He lay down, his color ashen.

"What's your name?" she asked.

The deputy fixed his gaze on her, and cleared his throat.

"Take your time, son," the doctor said.

"Shep Worley, ma'am."

"Do you have any kin?"

"Me and my wife live in Virginny City, Ma'am."

"Don't you worry. We'll get word to her." Lena hoped a letter would reach her in time.

In situations like this she wished they'd hurry up and finish putting up the telegraph lines. Big Jim could send a warning to the sheriff in Carson City that a gang of stage robbers and kidnappers were heading their way. Shep Worley's wife could be sent for so she could be here with her husband.

Shep began coughing again and flecks of pink foam ran from the corner of his mouth. Lena looked over at Dr. McKinnon.

The doctor hurried to his side. The coughing turned into a fit. The boy fell back and writhed on the table.

"Lena, go fetch the preacher," Dr. McKinnon said as he held the boy down so he wouldn't fall from his perch.

Lena backed away from the wounded deputy. Fear ruled the day but she wouldn't panic.

"I will bring him, Shep. You rest easy. You're in good hands with the doctor."

Lena left the room filled with grief and anger. She couldn't bear that Shep might die, especially away from his loved ones. The boy would need a miracle. She was a woman who believed in miracles.

The folks standing in the street stopped their chatter as Lena stepped out the front door of the cabin. They searched her face for news but Lena was in too much of a hurry to tell them all what she'd seen—a kid cut down in his prime by a hail of lead shot. A life shattered for a few thousand dollars in cash money.

Big Jim was the first to address her. "Did the deputy say anything more about the gang and which direction they were headed?"

"Let me pass. The doctor has called for the preacher."

Big Jim looked stricken with embarrassment. He'd been thinking about his payroll without any idea how bad the deputy had been hurt.

"Sorry, Lena." He stepped aside.

Lena planted her hands on her hips and addressed the crowd. "Now see here. You all should be organizing a posse to go after that gang. Henry Barrett already lit out of town on that black mule of his. He can't take on five armed bandits by himself."

"Let the sheriff in Carson take care of them," Mr. Andresen said.

"That's right," someone else in the crowd agreed. They all nodded in agreement.

"I've never known you to back down from a fight," she said to them.

The stagecoach driver removed his hat and held it over his heart. Big Jim scratched the back of his neck.

"Come on, Lena," Mr. Andresen replied. "There's none of us could catch the gang with a couple of hours' distance between us."

"What about the girl?" Lena asked. The men looked at each other.

She's shamed them in front of their women and children on purpose. Still, nobody stepped forward.

Lena shook her head. "As soon as I go and let the preacher know he's needed here, I'll be at the Carlson Mercantile. I'll put together a kit for any man willing to ride."

She searched each face for a response but they all looked away. For some reason, the gang had the whole town cowed.

"Don't take too long making up your mind," she said. "There's a girl's life at stake."

She gathered up her skirts and hurried as fast as she could to the church. Time was a wasting and she feared Henry and his daughter didn't have much time left.

Chapter Three

LENA STUFFED SADDLEBAGS with jerky and crackers and bags of ground chicory. As she worked, she recalled the determined look on Henry's face. He wasn't the kind of man who backed away when trouble came his way. She had to admire how he hadn't hesitated to light out of Ragtown when he found out his daughter was being held captive by a gang of ruthless stagecoach robbers.

Every man who owned a horse should be signing up to follow.

What this town needs is a sheriff of its own, Lena thought, a man who was willing to keep folks safe from these gangs that threaten their peace and prosperity. She knew exactly who'd fit the bill.

She was filling canteens with fresh water from a rain barrel when she saw a black mule walking down the middle of the street, saddle slipped sideways and bridle dragging in the dirt.

A freight wagon rumbled by and scared the mule up on to the rough-sawn boards of the boardwalk.

Mr. Belknap came out of his barber shop waving a willow broom at the beast but the mule had taken his post and there he planned to stay.

Lena hurried to help. Mr. Belknap cussed up a storm at the mule but the animal didn't budge an inch. She picked up the reins and gently coaxed him away from the safety of

Mr. Belknap's storefront. With a few more encouraging words, the mule stepped down off the boardwalk and back into the street.

"You got any idea who that mule belongs to?" Mr. Belknap held his broom in front of him in case the mule changed his mind.

"I think he belongs to Henry Barrett," Lena answered.

"Who?"

"The man who rode out of here this morning after the stage came through. He went after his daughter."

"The gal who was taken from the stage?"

"That's right."

Lena gave the saddle, blanket, bedroll and canteen a quick examination. Thankfully, she didn't see any blood. She shoved the saddle up on the animal's back and tied the reins around the pommel.

She cast Mr. Belknap a stern look. "I thought you were getting ready to ride posse and rescue her."

"Big Jim decided we'd better stay put. What if the gang didn't go to Carson? What if they come here to Ragtown?"

"Nobody's going to help Henry?" She put every ounce of her indignation into her words.

Mr. Belknap set the broom next to his red and white *Barber Shop* sign. "Now Lena, don't get yourself all riled. The town needs to be defended."

She was tempted to give Big Jim and the others a piece of her mind. A girl's life was at stake and Big Jim and the others didn't hold any conviction that something should be done to save her. It wasn't like the people of Ragtown to ignore somebody in need, but fear is a powerful thing.

"If this is his mule, then he's run into trouble," Lena said.

"You don't know that for certain," Mr. Belknap replied.

"Something happened for him and his mule to be separated." She didn't want to imagine what.

"A man like him can take care of himself," Mr. Belknap said.

Lena had thought so too but now she wasn't so sure.

"What should we do about this mule?" Mr. Belknap gave the beast an uncharitable look.

Lena took hold of his bridle. "I'll take him down to the livery."

"Boarding will cost two bits a day," he said.

Lena frowned. "The animal needs feed and water and the livery is the only place to keep him until Henry comes back."

"What if he don't?" Mr. Belknap asked.

Irritated at the shopkeeper's short-sightedness, she pulled on the mule's bridle and the animal followed her. Trying to convince Mr. Belknap of the rights and wrongs of the situation appeared to be a waste of precious time. Some men were born with their fists tight around their purses.

"I don't think the others on the town council will agree to pay for any stabling," he shouted after her.

"Don't worry," Lena replied over her shoulder. "I'll take care of the bill."

Her answer seemed to satisfy the man. He went back into his shop.

Lena led the mule down to the livery. Something had happened along the trail and the mule had found his way back to Ragtown along with Henry's gear.

What'd happened to Henry? What kind of trouble had he run into? There was no doubt in her mind that trouble had found him.

She was comforted that at least Henry had the Sharps to keep him company.

"HELLO?" LENA CALLED out. Morning light filtered through the cracks in the rough-sawn boards of the barn. She'd never been in the livery before. There hadn't ever been a need.

The livery owner, Lazarus Beaver, came out from behind a barrel-chested mare, a currycomb in his hand.

"Widda Carlson," he said, his voice full of gravel. He spat on the ground. "What are you doing here?"

"Brought you this mule. He belongs to a man who arrived this morning."

His gaze went to the mule. "I seen him. I seen him ride out of here, too."

"He took off for the men who robbed the stage," Lena said.

"All by his lonesome?"

"The girl who was kidnapped from the stage is his daughter. He rode out after the gang who took her." Lena nodded at the mule. "His mule's come back. I don't know what's become of him."

"Most likely those desperadoes bushwhacked him like they done the stage," the liveryman replied.

Lena feared the same, although there were other reasons why Henry might have become separated from his mule.

Lazarus took the reins from her. "If those men are bent on killing, they wouldn't spare any man who came after them."

Lena couldn't accept that Henry was dead. "What if

the gang didn't kill him?"

"What are you getting at?" Lazarus wiped his nose on his sleeve.

"What if they ambushed him and left him for dead."

"That's a possibility," Lazarus said.

"Somebody better go and find him. We can't leave him out there, dead or alive."

"I reckon you're right," Lazarus said.

"I'll pack saddlebags full of supplies and they're waiting at the Mercantile for anybody willing to go after Henry Barrett."

Lazarus started to unsaddle the mule. "I'll spread the word, Widda and I'll take good care of this critter."

"Thank you, Lazarus." Lena's mind churned. What had happened to Henry? Would anyone go after him?

Lena headed back to the store. A yellow dog lay stretched out in the shade of the boardwalk. He scrambled to his feet and followed her.

"Where do you come from?" She hadn't seen the hound around town before.

That yellow dog gazed with such devotion she had to smile.

She stopped and gave him a pat. He looked at mite thin and could use a bath, but otherwise looked sturdy enough.

"I suppose you're hungry?"

The dog barked.

"All right, then, come along," she told the dog. "I have an ox bone I could spare."

The yellow dog trotted alongside, his tongue hanging out one side of his mouth.

When they arrived at the mercantile, he sat by the door as she'd asked.

Lena unlocked the door and hurried inside. She'd no

time for customers so she left the Closed sign in the window and the shade drawn.

She sliced a chunk of fancy soap off a slab that had come all the way from Cincinnati, Ohio and wrapped it in brown paper. She opened one of Henry's saddlebags and stuffed in the soap and a plaster. Unfortunately, she had no willow bark elixirs in the store for pain or brown bottles of Dr. Coles for infection. Mr. Carlson hadn't approved of spirits and believed the bottles of medicine weren't drunk for their medicinal use anyway.

The dog was waiting and he thumped his tail against the uneven boards when he saw her. She tossed him a meaty bone which he set to with a hearty appetite.

Shading her eyes with her hand, Lena saw the empty streets and despaired. No one was coming to get supplies. No one was going to help Henry.

"I've never been a brave person," she said, "but I have to believe Henry's still alive and I can't leave him out there to fend for himself."

The dog jumped to his feet and began barking as if he understood every word.

"You any good at tracking?"

He kept up the ruckus.

"I reckon you could make yourself useful."

Lena went inside and lifted the heavy bag and flung it over her shoulder. She hung a canteen full of spring water around her neck.

She started off toward the livery with the dog at her heels.

Lazarus sat on an overturned box sopping a heel of brown bread in a pan of beans.

She dropped the saddlebag on the ground. "I need a horse."

"What?" The little man leaned forward as if he hadn't heard correctly.

"Henry Barrett rode out to find those robbers. Since he's not returned I have to consider the possibility he met up with them." She took a deep breath. What she was about to do defied all good sense. "He might still be alive. If he is, he'll need some help. Since nobody seems to be available, I'm volunteering."

Lazarus Beaver pushed back his sweat-soaked hat and scratched the sparse outcropping of hair on his head. "You best leave the finding of that miner fella to the menfolk."

"How long will it take for the menfolk to make up their minds?"

"Can't rightly say." Lazarus took a bite of his bread and chewed noisily. It appeared he didn't take her request seriously. "You know I'd oblige you anything you like, Widda, but you can't ride out of here looking for that girl's pa. There's a lot of places he might have gone. I'd be near next to impossible to find him, you not being experienced in such things."

"I'll take this hound with me. A dog with a good nose will cover a lot of ground."

Lazarus looked at the dog doubtfully.

"You know I wouldn't ask except a man's life could be saved," Lena said.

Lazarus sniffed. "Widda, you might as well face up to the fact that he's been mortally injured and there's nothing to be done. Besides, there's rain coming from the northeast and there's bound to be a lightning storm with it. You don't want to be out in that kind of weather if you can help it."

Lena swallowed the lump in her throat. She knew the territory was a harsh teacher and her chances of finding

Henry were slim. She couldn't leave him out there thinking nobody cared enough to come looking for him.

"Even if he's been killed," she told Lazarus, "I can't let the buzzards get him."

Lazarus set his empty plate on a barrel and stood. "Big Jim and the others will have my hide if they find out I let you ride out on your lonesome."

"You leave them to me," Lena replied with determination.

He walked away, shaking his head but talk of the buzzards had swayed him. When he returned he led a dun-colored mare by the bridle.

"This here is my best traveler," he said.

"She'll do, Lazarus," she said.

"You wait right here. I'll put a nice ladies' saddle on this gal."

Lena knew the type of saddle he meant. Mary McKinnon often rode with her husband when he doctored out to the Rocking J or Dory Jacobs needed delivering of another baby.

"Give me a regular saddle. I can't cover ground sitting sideways."

Lazarus had let her boss him around but her request had pushed him to his limit. He set his feet and folded his arms across his chest.

"Widda, I can't let you ride out of here looking like a cowhand. It ain't right for a lady to sit astride a man's saddle."

Lena had an idea. "I appreciate your concern for my reputation but you needn't worry. I'll be grateful if you'll lend me your trousers."

Lazarus' stunned expression would've made her laugh in other circumstances. She was dead serious.

"What do you want with my britches?" Lazarus hadn't liked what she was doing from the beginning and now he looked at her like she'd gone out of her mind.

"I need to wear them. You can't expect me to sit a horse with my drawers showing for all the world to see?"

"I hope you know what you're doing." He unbuttoned his trousers and let them drop to the ground. He wore a union suit that covered him from neck to ankles and needed a good washing. He didn't act self-conscious and there wasn't any need to be. Most folks around Ragtown considered her old enough to be their mother or older sister.

Lazarus tossed her his trousers and turned his back to give her some privacy.

"Thank you." She hiked up the scratchy woolen trousers and buttoned them. They fit tight around her hips and would split the seam if she bent over, but they would do.

She tied her shawl around her waist.

"You do look a sight," Lazarus said.

"I surely do," Lena replied.

Lazarus held back any more objections. He saddled up the horse like she'd asked, talking to himself while he did so.

"I'll be all right," she said when he'd finished.

Lazarus frowned. He knew as well as she did that what she was about to do could have dire consequences but he didn't know how to stop her.

He held the head of the little mare and Lena threw the saddlebag across its flank. The horse looked game but this wouldn't be any Sunday stroll.

Lazarus tucked a duster around the saddlebag. "It'll keep you dry."

She was touched at his concern for her well-being.

"Thank you, Lazarus. Thank you for all your help."

Lazarus huffed. No doubt, he'd catch an earful from the men in town when they found out what he'd done.

She placed her boot in the stirrup and pulled herself up. The horse shifted feet and Lena held on for dear life.

"Whoa, there," Lazarus said and he held the horse's bridle as Lena settled into her seat.

"What should I tell Big Jim and the others?" He looked up at her.

"Tell them I've gone after Henry Barrett. Hopefully, they'll follow."

"What if they don't?"

Lena considered this likely. "If I'm not back by morning, then I'll be needing help."

"What if nobody can find you?" he warned her.

"It won't come to that," she said, trying to sound confident. "Henry couldn't have gotten very far."

"Maybe you should take the mule."

Henry's mule stood in the corral munching his noonday meal.

"He's sure-footed and bound to come in handy in some of these out of the way places."

Lena shook her head. "He'll just slow me down."

She hadn't thought about what she'd do when she found Henry. If he was injured, he'd have to ride the mare. Lena would have to walk which would take hours for them to reach help. If he was dead, she'd bury him out there. Except she hadn't brought a shovel or anything else with which to dig the unforgiving earth.

She realized how unprepared she was.

"I won't bother with the mule but I'll need another one of your horses to bring Henry back."

The stableman nodded. "You just might."

As he saddled a second horse, Lena wondered if she was taking on more than she could chew.

Lazarus led the horse into the livery, her hooves clopping on the stone floor. He handed Lena the reins. His face was creased with worry.

"I don't mind telling you, I fear for your safety, Widda."

"I appreciate your help," she said. "I won't do anything foolish."

Whether she acted carelessly or courageously, only time would tell.

"God speed," he said.

Lena hesitated.

"You know how to ride?"

"I never learned. You'll have to give me a quick lesson."

Lazarus nodded. "Give her a kick to go and pull back on the reins to stop."

The directions seemed straightforward enough. "Like this?"

Lena tapped the animal's side with her boot and shook the reins. The mare took a couple of steps and stopped. The movement of the animal underneath surprised Lena. Riding a horse wasn't as smooth or comfortable as the wranglers and cowhands made it look when they came into town.

"Show that mare who's boss and you'll do fine," Lazarus said behind her.

Lena turned in her seat to look at him. Lazarus handed her the reins of the second horse. The reins secure, she was ready.

"Giddy-up," she said. She'd heard wranglers in town say this to their mounts.

The horse swished her tail.

"Widda, that horse knows you're afraid of her. She'll do what you ask if she knows you've got gumption."

Lazarus slapped the mare on her rump. Lena squeezed her legs around the horse's warm sides and gripped the pommel as they left the barn at a trot. The ride was bumpy and her whole body bounced in the seat. Lena was exhilarated. When they reached the main road, she pulled the reins and the horses stopped.

She saw Lazarus scramble off in the direction of the barbershop.

Lena called to the dog. He hurried to her side, his back end wagging like he hadn't seen her in ages.

"Henry went up this road," she told the dog. "I don't know how far he could've gotten on that old mule of his, but I need you to find him."

The dog looked in that direction.

"With fresh horses, we'll cover the ground in no time."

That yellow dog ran ahead until she couldn't see him anymore. Had he run off? Lena hoped not.

"As you well know, I'm new to riding, but I reckon I've gumption enough. We're going to have to get used to each other and find Henry Barrett."

She kicked the mare's round belly. The mare started walking.

The horses were good ones. They moved at a steady pace. The wind had kicked up, blowing tumbleweed across the road. Her mount's ears pricked forward but she didn't shy away or bolt.

Lena began to relax and enjoy the ride. The countryside was desolate but there was a beauty here that Lena had grown to love. The Sierra-Nevada mountains in the distance would be heavy with newly fallen snow soon.

They reminded her of home.

What would her papa say if he could see his little Lena, riding a horse and dressed in a man's trousers? She smiled because her papa was very strict about the behavior of his children. Mr. Carlson, God rest his soul, would never have let her do such a thing.

The territory wasn't as tidy as in the old country where rules had been made and followed for centuries. Women and men knew their place and no one objected. Out here, the rules didn't always apply. Maybe they needed new rules.

Lena couldn't help but ask herself why she would attempt a rescue in such an inhospitable land with uncertain success. She wasn't brave by any stretch of the imagination and what she'd taken on would need more courage than she knew she had. Someone had to find out what happened to Henry Barrett.

Chapter Four

THE DUN BURNED up the road at a steady pace. Lena held on for dear life, bouncing in the saddle. Grit soon coated her face and burned her eyes. She wrapped the reins of the extra horse around her hands and gripped the horse's mane, keeping her head down.

Several hours into the ride, Lena came to a place where an outcropping of jagged rocks provided ample cover for outlaws wishing to ambush anyone passing by. Who should be waiting for her but the yellow dog, tongue hanging out of the side of his mouth? She reined in her horse. Both horses came to a stop. The mare's sleek hide rippled, her energy not yet spent.

"Hello," she said to the hound. She surely was glad to see him.

He let out one sharp bark and disappeared behind a outcropping of rocks. Lena examined her surroundings with care. A sharp curve in the road with a sheer rock cliff to one side meant that a wagon or a stagecoach would slow passing this way.

The stagecoach driver had called the place where they'd been robbed Deadman's Creek. Lena listened but she didn't hear any water gurgling nearby. The long summer's drought had dried up the creeks weeks ago. Most likely Deadman's Creek was dried up too.

With the rocks for hiding places, she was struck at how

easy a robbery would be. She called out Henry's name and realized how foolish it was to announce her arrival.

What if the gang was close by, waiting on another victim? It was a possibility she needed to consider. Except the dog showed no particular interest in the hideaway behind the rocks which reassured her nobody waited there ready to pounce.

She dismounted and led the horses behind her. Plenty of tracks showed in the dirt but they could've been made by anybody. She continued around the rocks. Stubs of discarded smokes littered the ground. More than one man had waited here. She'd no doubt this was the place where the gang had robbed the stage and kidnapped the girl.

There was no sign of Henry.

She untied the canteen from its leather strap and drank a sip of water. The cool liquid satisfied her parched throat. The horses needed water. She hadn't planned on the creek being dry. It could be a fatal mistake.

The dog began to bark. The swirling dust made visibility difficult and she couldn't see him. She put the canteen back and put her foot in the stirrup. The mare side-stepped away from her. Lena grabbed the pommel before she fell.

"Now you wait a minute," Lena scolded. The horse looked back at her.

"You're going to stand still and I'm going to get up in the saddle," she said.

This time the mare didn't move as Lena pulled herself up and settled.

"I'm glad we understand each other." She patted the mare's neck.

The barking came from up in the hills, further away.

Lena picked up the reins and followed, ascending the steep grade carefully. The vegetation grew thick and tore at the hem of her skirt. Thankfully, Lazarus' trousers protected her legs. The horses needed urging as they stepped reluctantly up the gravel-strewn slope. When they reached a level spot, she pulled her horse to a stop and looked around. Even though the place was desolate, there was a rare beauty here. The pine and cedar gave the air a clean smell.

There was no sign of the yellow dog.

The sky rapidly darkened. Thunder rattled far off to the northeast. Rain would be here soon.

With a heavy heart, she realized Lazarus had been right. Henry could be anywhere in this vast wilderness. She'd no hope of finding him in bad weather.

Her horse stomped impatiently. She didn't want to be out here any longer. Of course, the mare would sense the danger of an approaching storm more quickly that Lena would. She turned the mare's head. She'd be lucky to reach Ragtown before the rain started.

She heard barking, closer this time. She couldn't leave without finding out what that fool dog had found and followed in the direction of the sound. The broken rock and loose soil made the climb slow and treacherous.

The yellow dog came out of the trees and began circling her, barking loudly. She dismounted, mindful of the rattlers that populated the territory. There was no mistaking the sound of a cartridge being shucked into a rifle's chamber.

Lena froze. She was exposed standing there without any cover but she called out anyway. "I'm Lena Carlson from Ragtown. Who's there?"

"What are you doing out here, woman?" a man's voice shouted back.

Lena's poor heart staggered a beat. It was the voice

she'd hoped to hear. She left the horses and climbed after the dog. In a depression in the ground with his back against a rock sat Henry Barrett. The Sharps lay across his lap. He'd tied his kerchief to cradle his left arm. His buckskin jacket was unbuttoned and his flannel shirt was torn.

Other than that, he seemed in passable good health. Lena was overcome with relief.

"Tell that mutt to quit his yapping." Henry scowled, looking like the devil himself.

"He's the one who found you," she replied. She reached over and patted the dog on the head. The dog stopped barking and lay down next to Henry. He rested his head on one of Henry's knees.

Henry ignored him. There was hurt in him that even an old yellow dog couldn't shift. Lena fetched the canteen from the pommel of her saddle and hurried back.

With black clouds hanging heavy overhead, she knew they didn't have much time before rain would make the journey back more treacherous than it already was. She fetched the canteen and hurried back to Henry.

He gulped a mouthful and wiped his mouth with his good hand.

"Most obliged," he said. He handed the canteen back to her and struggled to sit up straighter. He favored his right side. His face was a picture of regret as he did so.

"How bad are you hurt?" she asked, kneeling beside him.

"Shoulder's dislocated," he said gruffly.

"Did the gang ambush you?"

"My mule threw me."

Lena suppressed a smile. "Let me take a look."

"No need, I've taken care of it," he said. He tried to

push himself to his feet. He winced and fell back against the rock.

"Are you going to let me help, or are you going to pretend you're all right?"

Henry's eyes widened. Most likely, he hadn't expected her to talk back to him but Lena didn't have time to convince him what was best.

She eased off his kerchief and the buckskin jacket.

He squeezed his eyes shut as she unbuttoned his shirt and peeled it off his shoulder. It didn't take a doctor to tell her what they were up against. His shoulder and arm were in two different places and his arm hung limply at his side.

"I think I can put your shoulder back to rights."

"You ever set a shoulder before?"

"No, but I'm all you got."

He managed a thin smile. "I reckon that's so."

There wasn't any anger in his words, only acceptance. Lena was grateful he'd come around to her way of thinking.

Without any more fuss, she did what needed to be done. She took hold of his arm with both hands.

"What are you doing? You aim to torment me?"

"Don't worry. I saw Dr. McKinnon do this to a cow-hand who'd gotten kicked by a steer."

Henry took a deep breath, his face the color of ashes. She placed her boot against the rock face and jerked with all her might. Henry yelped. The joint popped back into place.

He straightened, rubbing his shoulder.

"How does that feel?" she asked.

He smiled at her weakly. "A whole lot better. Thank you kindly."

Lena felt a warmth spread through her.

She noticed blood on his neck. "Did you hurt your head?"

"Just a scratch. I hit my head on a rock when that mule threw me."

"Let me see."

He leaned forward and removed his hat. Blood had oozed from sizeable gash just above his ear. She hadn't brought a needle and thread but she had remembered to pack a plaster in her saddlebag. "I'll be right back."

"What are you going up to now?"

Lena let out an exasperated sight. "Dr. McKinnon will patch you up when we get back to town but right now I'll clean your head and put on a plaster to keep all this dust out of the wound."

She took the slab of soap from the saddle bag and poured precious water from her canteen on the cotton wool. The yellow lather worked into a froth and smelled strong, convincing her that the soap would do the job.

Henry shied away. She didn't try to convince him with words but knelt down and took hold of his head. The cut was deep. She dabbed gently but Henry stiffened each time she touched him.

"How long are you going to take?"

"Sit still, I'm almost done."

The yellow bubbles turned pink. When she doused the wound with fresh water, blood trickled down his neck. She didn't worry. The new blood would remove some of the dirt. She placed the plaster of cotton wool over the gash.

She needed a roll of cloth to secure the bandage.

Henry's shirt and kerchief were too dirty to use. She lifted her skirt and shrugged out of her petticoat. She began tearing the cotton into strips.

Henry looked like nothing she did would surprise him.

"What happened to Satan?" Henry asked as she wrapped his head with the strips of petticoat.

"What are you talking about?"

"My mule. Did you come across that mule?"

"He wandered into Ragtown. He's at the livery having his supper."

"I never did see a more stubborn critter than that mule."

She finished and tied the ends of the bandage. There was plenty of reason to believe that Henry and his mule were a lot alike. "There, I did my poor best but that should keep you until Dr. McKinnon has a look."

He touched the bandage gingerly and looked at her with gratitude. "You sure are a competent woman."

The compliment wasn't necessary but she realized, with a start, how good it felt to have him say so.

Henry snorted. "Who else's coming?"

"Just me and this yellow dog," she replied. "Folks fear the gang will come to Ragtown. The town will need defending if they do."

He tried to sit up straight but groaned from the effort.

"Take it easy," she said. She handed him the canteen.

He sat back against the rock and drank some more water. He was in a fair amount of pain and had lost some blood but there was plenty of fight in him. He would be strong enough to ride. She didn't need to tell him they had to get back to town before the storm hit.

"Did you pick up the gang's trail?" she asked as she stood.

He handed her the canteen. "Yes, and I know where they're headed."

"They're not going to Ragtown, are they?" She heard the fear in her voice.

He buttoned up his shirt. "There's no sign of them doubling back. As far as I can tell, they're moving west."

"We need a sheriff in our town. Nobody would try and rob the stage with a sheriff an hour's ride away."

"A sheriff's a tall order for any town," he replied.

Her mouth was dry as cotton but she gave Henry the few drops of water left in the canteen. He drank them greedily. They'd have to find more for them and the horses.

After he finished dressing, she helped him into his buckskin jacket. She'd hoped he'd warm to the idea of being their sheriff. She was sure he could do the job.

"Is it your habit," he asked, "to wear a man's britches?"

Had she detected a flicker of interest in his gaze?

"I couldn't very well ride all this way in a ladies' saddle," she replied.

"Mr. Carlson think kindly on your wearing pants?" There was a twinkle in his eye.

"Mr. Carlson is dead and has no say in the matter."

He averted his gaze. "I'm sorry, I didn't know you were a widow woman."

"It's been a long while." She stood. "Let's get moving."

Henry got to his feet, refusing her help. He took a step and staggered. Lena caught his arm and he shook out of her grasp.

"We've no time for your pride and right this minute you're in no condition to refuse a helping hand," Lena said.

She wrapped her hand around his waist, clutching to the buckskin jacket. Being so near him put her in a state of confusion. She'd tender feelings for him and she hoped they didn't show. She didn't want any awkwardness between them as they made their way back to town.

He weaved and she feared he would stumble.

She tightened her grip. The heat of his body and the scent of old leather competed for her favor.

He touched the side of his head. There was new blood on his fingertips.

"I'd hoped the bleeding had stopped," she said.

"Lucky I'm a hard-headed cuss."

She let him go when they reached the extra horse. The horses pawed the ground. They were ready to go.

He handed her the rifle. Using one hand, he pulled himself up into the saddle. Lena gave him his gun.

He shot her a lopsided grimace, hurting more than he would admit.

As she adjusted the saddlebag behind her saddle, she felt drops of rain on her face and shucked on Lazarus' duster.

"Rain's about to start," she said, looking up at the sky. "We're gonna get wet."

"Then we'd better hurry," he replied.

Chapter Five

THE RAIN PELTED them with cold fury, pushed by a biting wind. Henry led the way. She couldn't ride up beside him. The path was too narrow.

Luckily, he seemed to know where he was going.

Lena urged her horse to keep up but feared at any moment the mare would slip and fall. She needn't have worried about running short of water. A torrent of water rushed down the hill.

They'd been moving for over an hour and they still hadn't come to the main road.

Henry kept going, his head bent, his shoulders hunched against the cold. He kept the Sharps within easy reach across his lap.

She'd lost the feeling in the tips of her fingers and her hand cramped holding on to the reins. They had to stop and wait out this unforgiving weather. No doubt Henry would bulk but she couldn't go on much longer.

"We can't continue this way," she said, shouting above the noise of the storm. "You're worn out and so are the horses."

Henry pulled up. His horse didn't need any further persuasion to stop. Even the animals knew they should get out of this storm.

"I reckon you're right," he said.

She stood in her stirrups looking around for some shelter.

The wind made a frightful sound. A gust blew his hat off. They both were too tired to chase after it. The rain soon plastered his thinning hair to his scalp. His gaze was solemn but he wasn't frightened. His stubbornness and determination, she decided, were what they needed to survive.

"I came across a cattle puncher's hut along this trail. I think I can find it." He dismounted.

As he led his horse down the muddy, rock-strewn wasteland, Lena despaired. She feared they'd wander the countryside for hours looking for a place to wait out the rain. She'd no choice but to follow. After they'd gone on for another half hour or so she was ready to quit when she spotted the hut built into the side of a hill.

Henry headed in that direction. She guided her horse after him.

The little hut was solid built of stone. Henry removed the doorway made of willow branches. Lena dismounted and hurried inside. He ducked as he replaced the willow branches after her. The hut was six foot long and about half as wide. The air was heavily scented with wet earth and pine. Henry sunk to his knees. Lena stooped over to avoid tangling her hair in the nest of sticks that served for a roof.

There were no leaks or draughts, reason to be grateful but there was barely enough room for one person to sit down comfortably.

She saw, with relief, a kerosene lantern and a tin of dry matches. There was a bed roll and a few cooking utensils. Somebody used the cabin on a regular basis, a wrangler driving cattle into greener pastures come summer, most likely. She spread out the bedding for Henry.

She lit the lantern. It hissed and the smell of kerosene was strong but the lantern glowed warmth, a welcome commodity.

Henry removed his wet bandage. There was a red stain on the cotton.

"Your head is better?"

"The head is better."

With his fetching smile, he touched something deep inside her.

He sank back on the bedding. "I'm beholden to you, Lena. I'm a man who pays his debts."

This wasn't the kind of debt that needed to be repaid. He was a man, she thought sadly, who didn't trust the kindness of strangers.

"I'd better see to the animals." He started to get up. His grimace told her what he'd been trying to hide. He was in pain and couldn't have stood the travel much longer.

"You stay right where you are." She covered her head with her shawl and tied it under her chin.

She pushed away the tangle of branches. The rain came in frozen sheets of pure misery and flowed down the hills in tiny streams that widened until they joined together, creating a river.

She drew Lazarus' duster tight and bent her head against the deluge. She took up the reins of the horses and staked them on the side of the hut where the wind wouldn't reach them. She stripped off the saddles and wiped the horses with their blankets. The rubdown seemed to settle them. She filled the canteen from one of the streams running off a rock.

"I wonder what happened to that old dog?" she asked, looking around. She called out but only the wind answered. The dog had gone his own way and she was sorry for it. He'd led her to that ravine where she'd found Henry and she'd always be grateful.

Lena hefted her saddle and carried it to the entrance of the hut. She went back and did the same for Henry's saddle. Henry pulled both saddles out of the rain.

She picked up the saddlebag with their provisions and shoved it inside. Exhausted, she closed the makeshift door behind her.

Lena knelt down on the hard ground next to Henry. He shifted to give her more room but they were pressed together like sardines in a tin.

They were safe but soaked through. She couldn't stop shivering. She crossed her arms and hugged herself, aware of the heat coming from his body in the small space. If they held each other, they'd warm up faster but neither of them made a move to do such a thing.

Lena was as nervous as a maiden and had to laugh at herself for having such silly notions at her age.

"The yellow dog ran off," she said when her shivering had stopped and tiny pin pricks of feeling returned to her fingers and toes. She started to unwind her coronet braid.

"He probably headed back to town," Henry answered.

"I don't know where he came from," she said. "I never sae him before but he must belong to somebody."

"Reckon so," Henry said.

She stretched out her legs as much as she could and tried to get as comfortable as the tight surroundings allowed. As she finger combed her long tresses, Henry watched her. The moment was too intimate for strangers to share and she finished quickly.

Thunder shook the ground and Henry rose on one elbow. "Did you stake those horses?"

"I did. They'll be there come morning." Lena spoke

with a sense of satisfaction. She'd accomplished more than she'd thought possible of herself.

He sat back against the stone wall. "I'm not much help."

"You need to rest."

"Too bad there ain't any dry wood," he said. "A fire would sure feel good and a cup of coffee would be welcome on this cold night."

Lena pulled the saddlebags toward her. "I packed some jerky and crackers." She found the provisions and handed him some.

His eyes widened in appreciation. His mule had left him without food or water, and he must be starving. He bit off a piece of jerky and chewed.

Her thoughts turned to the girl. Was she huddled out somewhere in this miserable weather or did the gang have a hideout somewhere in these hills where they'd hole up for the night?

The possibility that the gang lurked nearby made her uneasy.

She looked at him to ask. He washed his jerky down with a drink from the canteen.

She hated to bring up this up but she had to ask. "Do you think the gang found shelter?"

"Most likely."

"Around here?"

"I don't know." He handed her the canteen.

"But you think so. That's why you were traveling off the main road."

"I'd tracked five horses as far as the place where you found me."

"Where are they headed?"

"I don't know. Maybe Carson Valley. Maybe they're

going all the way to California."

"You'll go after them."

"I mean to find my daughter."

"If she's like her papa, she'll find the strength to endure."

"I don't know if she's like me or not. I haven't seen her since she was a little girl."

"I know you'll find her," Lena said sincerely. "When you do, you two should get to know each other."

Henry pushed himself up further and settled back against the stones. "What I can't figure out is why she decided to come out here. There's nothing for her here and if she'd listened to her kin, she'd have been better off.

"Sounds like the girl made up her mind to be with her papa," she said. "You can't fault her for wanted to see you again."

"I reckon not."

"What's her name?"

"Her name's Caroline after her ma."

"I'll bet she's a very pretty girl."

Henry rubbed the whiskers on his chin. "More than likely. Her ma was a looker."

Lena caught his soulful expression as he remembered better days. Too bad he was dead set against the girl living in the territory. Lena felt certain he should give his daughter a chance.

"You don't suppose she's traveled all this way because she's had a falling out with her ma's people?" he asked.

"Are they difficult people to get along with?"

"No, they're fine folks."

"And your wife?"

He looked at Lena. "Her too but she's dead."

"I'm sorry."

He nodded. "This life out here was too hard on her. She didn't last. I sent my girl back to Missouri to be brought up proper."

"Now she's a lady."

"And too young to know what she's in for," he replied.

Henry reached inside his jacket and brought out a small envelope. He removed a piece of paper that had been folded and unfolded so many times the creases were torn.

"Her letter came last month on the Pony Express," he said. He read the letter one more time. "There wasn't time to send a reply. The trip from St. Jo takes three weeks by stage. She was already on her way by the time I received this."

He returned the letter to its envelope and tucked it back in his jacket. He found the bag of candy he'd bought that morning.

"This penny candy doesn't go with jerky but it's all the grub I have." His mood shifted. The light from the lantern sparkled in his eyes as he offered her the candy.

Lena took a lemon drop and popped it into her mouth. Her lips puckered but the sweetness of the candy satisfied. Henry shook out a piece from the bag for himself. He looked at it as if he hadn't seen candy in a great good while.

"Do you have children?" he asked.

"No. Mr. Carlson and I weren't blessed with any." Lena drew the duster closer, a chill passing through her. She'd accepted that God hadn't answered her prayers for children but the longing never went away.

"I hope you'll reconsider letting her stay," she told him. "You two should get to know each other and be a comfort to each other."

"That can't be," Henry replied. He put the lemon drop

in his mouth. "As soon as I rescue her from of those varmints who took her, she'll be on the next stage."

"Maybe you'll reconsider after you've seen her." Lena held on to a thread of hope.

"Not a chance."

"Why not?"

"The territory isn't the place for a woman. Living out here is just too difficult."

His remarks riled her. Henry surely had a low opinion of a woman's resilience. Lena had seen plenty of strong women along the trail making do with what little they had and enduring unimaginable hardship.

"There are plenty of women out here who'd prove you wrong," she said.

"The girl won't survive," Henry said testily. "The territory will break her like he did her ma."

Lena sighed. He'd made up his mind and nothing would move him away from his bull-headed opinions. She'd have to respect his decision even though she didn't agree with him.

She turned down the lamp. "Why didn't you return to the States with your daughter after your wife died?"

"I suppose I needed some time to myself." He slumped down. "Now Caroline's grown up. She'll be marrying soon and raising a family of her own. She deserves a better life than I could ever provide."

Henry shut himself away from family and friends grieving for a wife he still loved, Lena realized. His hurt ran deeper than the veins of silver that riddled these hills.

A love so strong it stayed with a man was a love to be envied.

It troubled her to think about her impending marriage to Mr. Kemp at the bank.

There was no love between them, only her practical nature and his ambition. All her life she'd believed love was a romantic notion reserved for stories in books. Henry Barrett had proved her wrong.

"Who looks after you?" Henry's question baffled her. Why did he care?

"At this moment, I look after myself. I have the Mercantile and an abundance of friends. What more do I need?"

She turned away as she lay down beside him. She didn't want him to see how she doubted the truth of what she'd just told him.

"You take the blanket," he said. "I've got my buckskin coat to keep me warm."

Before she could protest, he spread the blanket on top of her up to her chin. For a big man, he was extraordinarily gentle.

She choked up, his kindness affected her more than she could have imagined.

They lay side by side, sharing warmth in the cramped space, together and yet alone.

Lena couldn't sleep. She'd never slept next to a man before, not even Mr. Carlson who'd insisted on separate beds. Instead, she stared at the willow branches above her.

Henry was little more than a stranger and yet her body reacted to this man's touch in a fundamental way. She should be ashamed of herself and yet she wasn't.

One thing for certain, after tonight, they'd no longer be strangers.

When the rain stopped and the wind died down, Lena heard a familiar sound.

Henry Barrett snored while he slept.

Some women complain about the noise but Lena always found a sense of satisfaction from hearing a man sleep soundly, an inner peace that couldn't be bought with a pile of gold nuggets or a stack of territory bank notes.

As Henry slept, she took pride in what she'd done. She'd found him in a remote place thanks to the yellow dog. She tended his shoulder and patched up his head. She'd taken care of the horses and now him in the safety of this shelter. They were warm and dry and out of harm's way. The taste of sweet and sour candy still lingered in her mouth.

The night would soon be here. She wasn't about to wake Henry and suggest they head back to Ragtown.

Chapter Six

L ENA SAT IN the doorway of the hut. The air smelled clean. The sky had cleared to a crystal blue. The hills were gold in the first morning light. The horses grazed on what tufts of brush and whatever grass they could find.

Henry wouldn't have lasted out in the ravine last night. His mule had taken off with his provisions, leaving him with nothing but the Sharps and a handful of cartridges. He'd had no protection from the storm. She'd saved him from certain death. Henry seemed to appreciate her efforts. He'd called her capable. She took satisfaction from him saying so.

She'd spent a lot of time thinking during the night after she and Henry had talked about their families. She was beginning to know him as a husband and father. He'd loved completely and couldn't forgive himself for the death of his wife. He thought keeping his distance from his daughter would protect her.

Lena's marriage had been a success because she'd known its boundaries. Mr. Carlson had set the rules. She'd obeyed without question. They'd settled into a satisfying relationship because she knew what her husband expected of her.

Henry was a different sort of man. He was drifting with no purpose. He'd abandoned any rules to live by.

She wanted to reach him with words of comfort and

understanding.

All who'd come to the territory had suffered tragedy and terrible loss. Many had become separated from their loved ones by distances too great to imagine. She firmly believed it was up to those left to build up the community into a civilized place, to make something good from what had been lost.

He didn't want anybody's help, not even hers.

Blisters had gathered on her palms, a couple of them had broken open. She'd done a fair job of riding. She knew now what being saddle sore meant.

Where was that yellow dog this morning? They made a good team.

She whistled. There wasn't any response. Maybe Henry was right. Maybe the dog had found his way back to Ragtown and was waiting for her at the Mercantile. She hoped so.

She looked back at Henry. He slept with one leg propped against the wall of the shelter. There'd been an awareness last night that she had feelings for him. She'd been uncomfortable in such tight quarters. This morning Lena'd found herself curled up against him, using his broad shoulder for a pillow.

A tempest of mixed emotions brewed as she discovered something about herself. Something so personal her skin heated from thinking about it. It wasn't security she needed from a man but tenderness.

She heard barking and sat us. Who should come lopping her way but that muddy yellow dog. She rose stiffly. Yesterday's ride had taken its toll, leaving more aches and pains than she could count but she'd never felt more alive.

"There you are," she said. The dog jumped up on her. She laughed as she held his front paws and he barked.

"Look at you, you're filthy," she said sternly. The dog licked her face.

"Get down." She pushed him away. The dog shook himself off and sat at her feet.

She reached down and patted his head. "I'm glad to see you."

"That hound looks like he'd been hunting the better part of the night." Lena turned to see Henry crouched in the doorway.

"Too bad he didn't catch a rabbit," Henry said. "We could use some grub."

The dog's tail thumped on the ground as if he understood every word said.

"I've got a big bone waiting for you," she told the dog, "as soon as we get back to Ragtown."

"As for you," she said as her gaze met Henry's. His eyes were smudged with fatigue but otherwise, she had to admit, he looked better than a man ought to first thing in the morning. "How are you feeling?"

"Tolerable," he said.

"Does your shoulder hurt?"

Henry stood. "Some."

"I'll get a fire going and start some coffee," she said.

"Don't bother on my account. We've got some ground to cover this morning."

"I'm ready when you are." She waited for him to move aside so she could take collect the saddlebag. The awkwardness between them had returned.

Henry used the Sharps as a walking stick. He didn't ask for help and she didn't offer any. He looked old and tired as he moved off to do his morning constitutional. His body had suffered more than he was willing to admit.

Lena dragged the saddlebag out in the open. She also

was restless to start back for town.

Besides getting Henry to the doctor, she wanted to know what news there was of the outlaws. Henry had followed their trail going west but the gang might have changed their mind and headed for the shelter of a town. Ragtown would've been the closest.

Lena worried. The town hadn't had a gunfight in years. The row of saloons attracted cowboys, freighters and teamsters but for the most part, those men kept their drinking inside the confines of those establishments and their disagreements to a minimum. On Sundays, church was full and the collection plate mounded with silver dollars. Since the Comstock, a different breed of men roamed these hills, filled with greed and willing to kill for easy riches.

She worried about young Shep Worley and whether he'd died from the bullet delivered by the gang. She worried about Henry's daughter. Had Caroline Barrett survived the night?

Lena was convinced, more than ever, that Ragtown needed the presence of the law to keep order. Big Jim and the others must be persuaded, and she would be the one to do it as she and Henry returned.

HENRY PICKED UP her saddle with his good arm and rested it on his hip. With strength and will, he hefted the saddle on to the horse's back. He was tough, no one would argue. She'd experienced another side of him. He was a man who could be gentle.

Lena had to wonder what kind of work he did before he became a placer miner with a black mule his only company.

He hadn't spoken of his daughter this morning. He hadn't shared with Lena what he thought her chances were now that she'd been missing since yesterday. Lena didn't want to think what might have happened to a girl of seventeen held prisoner by a gang of desperate men.

Without a word, he saddled his horse. At last they were ready. Without a word, Henry mounted his horse. Lena climbed aboard the mare who stood perfectly still.

They rode slowly down the rain-slicked side of the hill. The tracks of man and beast had been obliterated by last night's deluge. Henry kept his eyes to the ground anyway. He was a man determined to pick up any sign of five men riding. She knew he wouldn't give up until he found his girl.

Lena had left her hair down. Gusts of wind blew the tendrils across her face but she didn't mind. She felt like a girl of twenty again.

At last she saw the main road below them. It was the first sign of civilization they'd come across since they left the wrangler's hut. Even though she'd no regrets coming out here to fetch Henry, she'd be glad when they arrived back home.

As they approached the main road, she heard rumbling off to the east. She looked at Henry who'd heard the noise and squinted in that direction.

She strained to see who was coming.

"Why, it's Lazarus," she said.

The liveryman drove a buckboard. When he saw them, he reined in his horses. The buckboard creaked and groaned to a stop. He spat over the side as he waited for them to travel the last fifty yards.

"Thank the Lord," he said when they arrived. "I'm

mighty glad to see you, Widda Carlson."

Lena could say the same.

Lazarus looked at Henry. "You must be the fella she went after."

"Henry Barrett."

"Pleased to meet you. I'm Lazarus Beaver. I own the livery in Ragtown. Those horses you're riding come from my stable."

"He loaned me the horses and his britches," Lena added.

"Yes, siree," Lazarus said with a measure of self-satisfaction. "The widda made a strong argument that you might be alive."

"Don't that beat all," Henry said.

Lena smiled. "I'd told Lazarus to come looking for me if I didn't return by morning."

Lazarus looked rueful. "I'd have been here last night but the bad weather kept me inside."

"No need to apologize," Lena said. "We found a stone hut not far from here. We're none the worse for wear."

"I'm sure glad to see you safe and sound. Everybody in town's worried about you." Lena couldn't help but be proud. The people of Ragtown worried about her. She'd been missed and fretted over.

She turned to Henry. "Lazarus took in your mule."

Henry leaned against his pommel. "I'm much obliged."

Lazarus nodded. "Don't thank me. The widda said she was good for the animal's fare."

Lena got off her horse. "Let's not waste time talking about that mule. Any news about the gang?"

"None and I can tell you, folks are plenty scared."

Henry shifted in his saddle as she tied her mount to the back of the buckboard. Lena climbed on board and sat down next to Lazarus. She'd had enough riding for a while. The yellow dog jumped in the back. Apparently, he'd the good sense to ride rather than walk.

"Let's get back to town," she said to Henry. "You can get fresh supplies and have the doctor look at your head."

Henry looked down at her. "I'm not going with you to Ragtown."

Lena didn't believe what she'd just heard. Not even Henry Barrett could be that hard-headed. "Don't be an old goat. You can't travel in your condition."

"I'll be just fine."

"You can't go after her by yourself."

He scowled, a bad habit she was beginning to understand. He grew easily aggravated when contradicted.

"Who's man enough to ride with me?"

"We're all afraid for your girl." Lena meant to reassure him but knew her words fell short.

"There isn't a posse coming." There wasn't blame in his voice, only recognition that nobody saw fit to come after them except Lazarus.

"I know," she said. "Like I told you, there isn't anyone willing to leave Ragtown undefended."

Unfortunately, his years out here in the territory had taught him folks couldn't be counted on.

"You'd better take my saddlebags," she said. "There are a few things left that you'll be able to use."

His gaze warmed her. "Thanks to you I won't starve."

Lena returned his gaze with an affection she made no effort to hide. His confidence settles her worries. The man knew how to calm nervous horses and feisty ladies. She would have never guessed, looking at him, he possessed such a skill.

He removed the saddlebag from her horse and flung it

across the back of his mount.

She looked at Lazarus. The store needed tending. She'd neglected her customers long enough.

"We'd better get started," she said.

Lazarus shook the reins and they moved forward. He turned the buckboard around in the rutted road. She held on as the buckboard rocked but Lazarus knew what he was doing and it didn't take long before they were on their way home.

"Hold up," she said to Lazarus.

They came to a jolting stop.

She turned in her seat and saw Henry riding away. Although his head must hurt and his shoulder must be aching, he sat tall in the saddle. There was a quiet dignity to him, a man who had a job to do.

"He'd make a good sheriff," she said.

Lazarus nodded. "I was thinking the same."

Henry's departure upset her. What created a frenzy of indecision was that she wanted to go with him.

Papa had picked Mr. Carlson to be her husband, a man twenty years older than she was. He'd wanted for her to marry a man who'd give her security. She'd obeyed her papa because a good girl did as she was told.

When Mr. Carlson had decided he wanted to go to America for a better life, Lena didn't question his decision.

They'd left their old world roots and sailed across choppy seas. They'd joined a wagon train in Independence, Missouri. The arduous journey across the plains had been a trial of agonizing hardship. They'd met up with Indians, disease and unbelievable heat but she'd survived. By God, she had.

Now she was on her own and wasn't accountable to any man. She could make up her own mind.

She climbed down from the wagon and untied her horse.

"What are you up to?" Lazarus raised a brow.

"I can't let him go on alone."

Lazarus' face puckered. "What'll I tell folks back in town?"

"I don't know," she answered. Lena had always been so level-headed and practical-minded. She wasn't being herself and Lazarus knew it.

The yellow dog stood up, ready to join her.

"You'd better go back with Lazarus," she told the hound. "No telling what me and Henry will come across."

Thankfully, the dog understood the wisdom of her request and he sat down.

Lena climbed into the saddle and picked up the reins.

"How long will you be?" Lazarus asked.

"I can't tell you how long we'll be or even if we'll have any success. I just know this is something I have to do."

"I reckon that'll be enough for folks." Lazarus touched two fingers to the brim of his battered hat.

Lena gave her reins a shake and started off. It didn't take long to catch up with Henry.

"I'm coming with you," she said, as she drew along side of him.

He shook his head. "I can't let you."

"Why not?" She deserved more of an answer after saving his life. "I can ride. You know I can."

"There'll be shooting."

"Two against five is better odds in my book."

"I can't let you come along. I don't want to be responsible for you getting hurt."

"You can't stop me."

Henry's face bunched up into a frightful scowl. Time

he found out that all women didn't break at the slightest bit of discomfort.

Before he could take off, Lena leaned over and grabbed the bridle of his horse. The mare stepped back but Lena held on firmly. All her life she played the hand she was dealt. But not this time.

Henry Barrett was going to listen.

"I'm not a wrangler and I'm not accustomed to sitting a horse but I'm capable, you said so yourself. I'm a hard worker and did a fair job patching you up. Seems to me out here where the land needs taming and the law's neglectful, a woman like myself would be useful."

She let his horse go having said her piece. What she'd told him struck at the core of the matter. He could depend on her.

"Lena," he said, using her given name for the first time. "You're the peskiest woman I ever did come across."

She knew he spoke honestly and from the heart. Her eyes stung with tears. It was the nicest compliment she'd ever received.

He smiled, by Lord in Heaven, he did. She was smiling too.

"I suppose if I don't let you come along," he said, "you'll just follow me anyway."

"I'm glad we're beginning to understand each other."

His mouth twitched. His blue eyes held her like an embrace. Lena liked what she saw.

LENA AND HENRY rode side by side each cocooned in their own thoughts.

They came to the road due north that lead to Virginia

City. Continuing on would take them to the territory's capital, Carson City. Beyond Carson City lay the Carson Valley and across the mountains was California.

Henry studied the ground but the road hadn't been traveled since last night's rain.

Lena sat back and looked around. She didn't like this place. There were too many places to hide.

"They could be anywhere," she said.

"They're headed for Virginia City."

"How can you be so sure?"

"They've got money in their pockets and Virginia City is a good place to spend it with no questions asked."

Lena understood his meaning. Ever since silver ore had been discovered at the Comstock mine, there'd been amazing wealth in the town. Nobody would bat an eye at a bunch of fellows spending cash freely.

He turned his horse's head in that direction. Lena did the same. There'd be no further discussion. Henry knew the territory better than she did and he'd made up his mind.

"How long before we reach Virginia City?" she asked.

"A couple of hours if we're lucky." He took a deep breath. "There's six miles of bad road ahead, mostly going uphill."

"What if the gang's not there?" Going north would take valuable time if he'd guessed wrong. It was a possibility they needed to consider.

"We'll move on," he said.

They climbed the well-worn road. Pines forested both sides, growing tall toward the sun. After an hour, they dismounted and walked, giving their horses a rest.

Lena saw tiny fingers of smoke just beyond the next ridge. She looked at Henry.

He'd seen the smoke. They stopped to think about the implications.

"Do you think those outlaws camped out in the rain last night?" she asked.

"Could be." He dismounted and handed her the reins to her horse. He tucked the rifle under his arm, and then put a finger to his lips. She slid to the ground and led both mounts. As they came closer to the smoke, Henry motioned for her to stay put with the horses.

Lena had no objection doing as she was told.

Henry crouched down and approached the campfire without making a sound. When he reached a boulder, he stood and looked around. Her heart pounded and her legs felt like they were made of jelly. She didn't know if she'd be able to run or not if there was shooting.

After a few minutes, he motioned for her to follow. She led the horses to where he waited. There was no sign of activity. No laughing or talking. No horses were staked nearby. The place was eerily silent except for a sound she recognized.

Flies had started a meal on whatever was in that camp.

As she drew nearer, she saw two people sprawled on the ground. A dead pack mule loaded with mining tools lay on its side.

"This one's dead," Henry said, turning the man over with his boot.

"So's this one," she replied. The body in front of her lay face down in the dirt. Part of the skull was missing. Blood had soaked into the ground. Brains and bits of bone were infested with black flies.

Lena looked up at the sky and tried to breathe normally. She had never seen such an act of violence and for what purpose? She wanted badly to leave but what use would she be to Henry and her girl if she couldn't manage this awful sight?

"They haven't been dead for long," Henry said.

She forced her gaze downward. The two men wore jackets made out of buffalo hides. Their raccoon caps had fallen off in the dirt. Their bodies were yards from their campfire. They'd been trying to escape whoever had intruded on their camp.

She found one of the men's packs spread out on the ground. Their possessions had been scattered. All that was left were two tin cups, a coffee pot and a worn Indian blanket. There were no weapons and no sacks of gold or silver.

She picked up the blanket and covered the smaller man. His expression was frightful. He'd known what was coming.

"Do you think the gang did this?" she asked.

"Could be." Henry crouched down and picked up a handful of dirt. "There are a number of prints made by horseshoes in this camp. I'd say four or five mounts."

Lena shook her head. Her grief had turned into anger. "Not a fair fight. These two men didn't have a chance."

"Reckon whoever raided these boys did so for the gold or silver they were carrying."

"Why'd they kill the mule?" she asked. "They could've got a good price for a mule, especially this close to the Comstock."

"The critter must've been caught in the crossfire," Henry said, soberly.

"I expect that's what happened," Lena agreed.

Henry stood and brushed off his hands. "They're moving north but they're walking their mounts.

"It must be the gang," Lena replied. "Caroline is slowing them down."

She hoped the gang hadn't done this evil thing. She didn't want to think about Caroline witnessing such dreadfulness.

Henry picked up one of the dead men's picks and started digging under the shade of a tall pine tree.

They buried the two men. Lena said a few words memorized from the Bible. Henry held his hand on his chest, his gaze as hard as steel.

The outlaws who'd wreaked this havoc were bold and ruthless, murdering two men in cold blood. Men who could do this must be caught and put in jail.

Henry and Lena packed up the men's belongings to take to Virginia City. Someone, somewhere wondered and worried about these two. The sheriff would make sure the families received what was left of their gear and tell them of their loved one's fate.

They continued up the road. There was more urgency to their pace than before. Two men had been killed minding their own business. How many more would meet the same fate? Lena worried there'd be more killing before the day was done.

They hadn't gone much farther when they saw another reason to be alarmed.

A carcass of a horse, bloated and stinking to high heaven, lay by the side of the road.

Henry leaned forward in his saddle. "Shot thought the head."

"Broke its leg," Lena replied. The poor animal's front leg was bent at an odd angle. She'd seen worse but she never got used to the sight. The animal must've suffered horribly.

"Do you think it's the same men who killed those prospectors?" she asked.

"I'm thinking there's a good possibility. They're short a horse and riding double on two now," Henry said.

"They can't be far ahead," she replied.

"We'll catch up with these desperadoes in Virginia City." He gave his horse a kick. "Let's ride."

BEFORE LONG, LENA heard the steady pounding of the stone crushers at the silver mines. The ground shook in a steady rhythm.

They arrived in Virginia City, a town sprouted up not far from where silver had been discovered by two Irish lads two years ago and named the Comstock Lode. She marveled at the new construction everyplace she looked. The hills were a whirlwind of activity with newly dug mine shafts and equipment scouring the bowels of the earth for silver ore.

People from all walks of life crowed the mud-caked streets. They'd built the main street along a ridge with a view that beggared description. There were more saloons than she could count and in some places a church alongside them. There was a mercantile on every block. There was even an Opera House, a place Lena had never been but she thought it a sure sign of civilization to have one.

Henry rode ahead as Lena gawked at more sights of the bustling town. She saw women in silk dresses and carrying fancy parasols. She saw men in black suits and shiny boots. There was money spent up here from fortunes that went beyond the imagination. Not only did the mine owners prosper. She'd heard a man with a strong back could make four dollars a day mining these hills, four times what a man made in the old country doing the same job.

A woman dressed in black caught Lena's eye. She was handing out leaflets to those who'd take one.

Lena stopped and reached out for one. The woman's face was pinched and disagreeable. She gave one of her leaflets to Lena but she didn't meet Lena's gaze.

Lena supposed wearing trousers had a lot to do with the woman's disapproval. There was no time to explain.

The broadside was from the Ladies' Temperance Union. It described the evils of drink and the consequences of drunkenness. Lena wondered how these ladies fared in a community with so many saloons and if they'd made any progress.

Henry was already a few blocks ahead of her. He stopped and dismounted in front of a brick building. She urged her horse forward to join him.

A man half Henry's age, his chair tipped back against the wall, whittled on a block of wood in front of the jail. He wore a tin star pinned to his chest. When he caught sight of Henry, he almost tipped over.

"I'll be a skunked dog," he said, scrambling to his feet. "If it ain't Henry Barrett."

"Morning, Charlie." Henry threw his reins over the hitching post.

Lena was surprised the two men knew each other but she was reminded there was a lot about Henry Barrett that she didn't know.

The Virginia City sheriff was bowlegged and stiff from sitting. "Ain't you a sight for sore eyes?" He reached out with an eager hand. Henry shook it amiably.

"What are you doing in these parts?" the sheriff continued, folding his knife and stashing it in the pocket of his trousers. "Last I heard, you were working a claim near

Unionville."

"You heard correctly. I come looking for a gang of five men who robbed the stagecoach headed for Ragtown yesterday. They took a cash box with wages from the Rocking J. You make any arrests in the last twenty-four hours?"

The sheriff scratched his chin. "A couple of miners shooting their weapons in the city limits. They'd struck a vein of silver and saw fit to celebrate."

Henry shook his head. "This gang has a girl with them."

Lena cleared her throat.

Both men turned and looked at her.

She noticed the cold determination she'd seen in Henry's eyes earlier. Yesterday it would've frightened her. Today she drew strength from his steadfastness. Henry wouldn't quit until he found his daughter.

"Charlie Maynard, this here is Mrs. Carlson."

"Hello Sheriff, you can call me Lena. All my friends do."

"Please to meet you, ma'am." Sheriff Maynard remembered his manners and removed his hat and bowed.

Lena liked him instantly.

"You two come on in and I'll make a fresh pot of coffee."

"No time to waste socializing," Henry said. "I'm here for those outlaws and I mean to find them."

"What makes you think they're in Virginia City? There's been no report of an outlaw gang hereabouts."

Henry scowled. "Lena and I come across two men killed about an hour's ride from here. I counted five horses leaving their camp. They hadn't been dead long and whoever did it was heading this way."

The sheriff's expression turned hard. As glad as he'd been for the company, Lena decided, he put his job first and foremost.

"I'll ride out there. You can show me where they're at."

"We buried them, Charlie. This here is their gear." Henry showed the sheriff the two packs.

"You think the culprits are the same bunch that robbed the stage?"

"I'm not sure but I aim to find out. The girl with them is my daughter."

"You mean little Caroline?"

"She's not little anymore, Charlie."

The sheriff shook his head. "How'd she come to be with a gang of desperadoes?"

"They took her as a hostage," Henry said.

The sheriff let out a whistle. He looked mighty unhappy.

"The gang dry-gulched the stage at Deadman's Creek and wounded a deputy," Henry said.

"That'd be Shep Worley. Was he hurt bad?"

"We don't know," Lena answered. "He's in good hands with our doctor. He told me he has a wife up here."

"I'll get word to her right away. Why in the heck didn't anybody let us know?"

"Nobody could be spared," Lena explained. "We're afraid the gang will come to our town."

Charlie brushed dust off his hat and squashed it on top of his head. "I'll ask around if anybody's seen strangers in town with a girl riding with them. It shouldn't take long to find out where they're holed up, if they're still in town."

"Those outlaws are on a murderous rampage, Charlie, and I've got to stop them." Henry picked up his reins. "I'm heading for the saloons. That's most likely where they went off to."

"Now you hold off, Henry. There are one hundred and twenty saloons in this town. You'll need help."

Henry scowled.

Charlie didn't back down. "This here is my town. You won't be taking on anybody by yourself."

"You never were one to mind your elders," Henry said.

"You stay here, Lena," Charlie said, grinning. "Me and Henry will take care of the gang."

"No sheriff, I've come this far and I mean to stay with Henry."

"A gunfight's no place for a lady," Charlie said. He looked at Henry. "If it comes to that."

"So I've been told," Lena said.

"It's no use, Charlie, she'd dead set on helping." Henry had a glint in his eye.

"I can't guarantee your safety, ma'am," Charlie said.

Lena smiled. It was a man's natural inclination to protect a woman but Henry Barrett recognized she'd as much conviction as he had when it came to making things right.

And now so did young Charlie Maynard.

Chapter Seven

WORD CAME FAST to Sheriff Maynard that five men were spending money fast and loose at a place called the Gentlemen's Drinking Club.

Lena hadn't been sure that they followed the same men who'd robbed the stage and taken Caroline but her spirits soared when the messenger told Charlie about a lady being with them.

They had no trouble finding which saloon the gang had favored in a town full of salons. Four spent horses, their heads drooping from a hard ride, were tied out front.

In no time, Charlie had the Gentlemen's Drinking Club surrounded by armed men. He posted a boy named Joseph to deter traffic to another road while he handled this arrest. Two men occupied second story windows across the street, their long guns ready. Two others hid behind a freight wagon ten yards up the street.

Charlie directed Henry and Lena to take a position at the corner of the two story building to the left of the saloon. Lena admired his confidence and organizational skills. Nothing was left to chance.

"I'll go in," Henry told him.

"I appreciated the offer but this is a job I'm paid to do," Charlie replied.

Henry put his hand on Charlie's shoulder. He was old enough to be Charlie's papa and he looked at him with pride at the man he'd become.

"Then I guess I'd better let you," Henry said.

Charlie started off in the direction of the saloon, walking like a sailor on a ship in high seas. He bad legs didn't slow him down. There was confidence in his walk Lena decided, and purpose.

Henry guided Lena to the corner. The building provided some shade. She could hear a piano playing and laughter.

Opening the breech on his rifle, Henry checked his load. He didn't take any chances either. These were desperate men who'd already killed two men. Arresting them wouldn't be easy.

"You didn't tell me you knew the Virginia City sheriff," she said, trying to keep the fear out of her voice.

Henry closed the breech and watched Charlie. "I knew his ma and pa a long time ago. His pa and I rode with General Richardson. We fought Indians together when we were young bucks."

"What made you give it up?"

"I met Caroline's ma and I quit my fightin' ways."

Lena settled back against the rough-sawn boards of the building. She understood why he'd lost his bearings and lived alone, rejecting companionship except for his black mule.

Charlie Maynard stood about twenty feet away from the entrance of the saloon. He'd withdrawn his six-shooter from its holster and aimed at a pair of batwing doors painted barn red.

Henry stepped out from behind the building and raised the Sharps. He aimed at the doorway. Lena waited, protected by the building, wishing there was something she could do.

"You boys come out with your hands up," Sheriff Maynard shouted.

The piano playing stopped. Chairs scraped across hardwood floors and people moved about inside the saloon.

Lena watched the exit. Would the gang come out willingly and surrender? She looked at Henry. The man itched for a fight. He was ready and willing to take on those men in the saloon to rescue his girl.

She heard glass breaking. A hail of bullets exploded from inside the saloon. Charlie fired his six-shooter. A blast rang out from the Sharps and from the other shooters in the sheriff's posse. The acrid smell of gunpowder filled the air.

Charlie hit the ground and fanned his gun as he rolled. The men in the saloon returned fire. One of the men in a second story window clutched his chest and fell against the window frame. His rifle rattled down the rough-sawn shingles and landed in the street.

Henry scrambled back to the corner of the building. Charlie Maynard found shelter behind one of the town's watering troughs.

"You hit?" he shouted to Charlie.

"Naw, how 'bout you?"

"Missed me too, but you lost one of your boys in the window behind you."

Charlie glanced behind him and then returned his gaze to the batwing doors. Henry ejected the spent shell and reloaded.

"They won't let you take them alive," she said, handing him a cartridge. She'd stated the obvious but she had to say what Henry needed to hear. He could be single-minded when it came to getting a job done.

"So be it. We'll have to kill every last one of them."

Lena shuddered, remembering those two dead miners and what happened to their mule. "If Caroline's inside the saloon with those men, she could be in the line of fire."

"There's no other way, Lena."

Charlie finished reloading and pumped more bullets into the saloon. Both windows shattered. Henry stepped away from their hiding place and fired. His aim was steady and true. One of the saloon doors swung on a broken hinge.

A fresh volley of gunfire came from the saloon. Henry retreated, breathing hard. He shucked the spent shell.

"This could take days," she said.

Henry hurriedly reloaded and closed the breech. "They'll get tired. They'll start bickering with each other, then fighting. We'll close in and finish them off."

"Somebody needs to get inside," she said. An idea had come to her but she needed Henry's support.

"The gang will murder anyone who gets halfway close."

"Maybe they'd let me in."

He turned and fixed her with a lethal gaze.

"I'll go dressed as one of those Temperance Union ladies looking for collections."

His eyes were vivid and his anger clear. "No, you won't."

"They won't consider a Temperance lady a threat."

"Threat or not, I'm not discussing it," Henry said.

Lena's temper flared. "I think it would work."

"I can't let you go in there. Those men are looking to do some more killing."

Lena knew the Virginia City Gentlemen's Club was a dangerous place but it was Henry's commanding tone that put a burr under her collar.

"Henry Barrett, I've made up my mind to go into that saloon."

Henry's face crinkled up like the old goat he was. A lot of years lined that face and she loved every one of them, but he hadn't figured out the ways of womenfolk and she reckoned experience was the best teacher.

She stood on her toes and kissed his cheek. The moment was too precious and uncertain not to. Henry kissed her back with a scratchy kiss square on her lips.

All those years of loneliness seemed to fly away. She thought of all she'd missed. When he stopped, she was breathless. Her passion ran deeper than she'd ever imagined. Her feelings weren't comfortable or settled but scary and reckless like those boys in the saloon.

They'd have to deal with these feelings later. She prayed there'd be a later.

He held her by the shoulders and looked square in her face. "I can't lose you."

"You won't." She put her hand on his chest. She could feel the beating of his heart.

"What about Charlie? He's a sitting duck out there." She knew he wouldn't let any harm come to the boy.

Henry looked over at Charlie Maynard crouched behind the watering trough. They both knew he couldn't stay there the rest of the day.

He turned back to Lena. "I'm going out and cover him. You stay put."

"Be careful."

He hitched a stray hair behind her ear. This small consideration gave her goose flesh right down to her toes.

Henry let her go and dashed from their hiding place. A bullet ricocheted off the dirt two feet in front of him.

Lena's throat tightened. He slid into the safety of the watering trough as Sheriff Maynard emptied another round into the saloon.

He looked back and gave Lena a quick salute.

While the two men palavered, Lena headed in the opposite direction.

IN A TOWN populated mostly by men, a woman stood out. A woman dressed in black passing out leaflets in front of a saloon couldn't be missed.

Lena found the Temperance Union worker they'd come across earlier a few blocks away from the standoff. She looked to be about the same size and height as Lena. She gazed at Lena with suspicion as she thrust a leaflet into Lena's hand.

"What are you doing out on the boardwalk?" Lena asked. "There's a shootout down at the Gentleman's Drinking Club."

"Certainly the sheriff won't let the situation come this way," she replied in a crisp voice.

"The situation?" Lena replied. The woman had no understanding about the danger she was in.

The Temperance Union lady looked her over with obvious distaste. "What would you call it?"

"I'm sure the sheriff appreciates your confidence," Lena replied sharply. "There are five very bad men ready to escape or die trying."

She stiffened. "What, may I ask, are you doing in the street?"

"I've come to ask you a favor."

"What kind of favor?" she asked with suspicion.

Lena outlined her plan. "It'd be a great service to the community if you'd lend me your costume and bonnet."

"Are you sure it would work?" the woman asked. "You'd be taking a terrible risk."

"I'm not sure but it's a chance I'm willing to take to save a girl's life."

The woman blinked. "I do believe those outlaws would be in for a surprise."

Lena smiled.

"Come with me." The Temperance Union lady started off down the boardwalk.

Lena learned her name was Mabel. Her husband and three children had died from the fever coming across the plains from St. Louis. She had been in the Comstock for three months and boarded with a dressmaker. The Temperance Union folks gave her enough money for handing out their pamphlets so she didn't have to work in the saloons.

Mabel took Lena to the dressmaker's place to change her clothes.

Lena stripped off her own clothes and the trousers. Mabel stepped out of her black skirt and untied her petticoat. The petticoat, made of flour sacks, had been heavily starched.

Under a black garter, she wore a tiny pistol. She removed the gun and handed it to Lena.

"There's only one bullet but at close range it'll kill a man."

Lena shook her head. Killing a man hadn't been part of the plan.

"Go ahead," Mabel said. "It's the only persuasion some men understand."

Lena took the weapon. It fit neatly in her hand. "Carrying a pistol will be a first for me."

Mabel shivered as she stood in her linen slip, tightening the bone corset for Lena.

Lena never had a figure that would be considered fashionable but after Mabel finished, she had to admire herself in the mirror. Her waist had shrunk and her lily-white bosoms showed prominently. The full skirt ballooned out all around her. The jacket didn't button, however, and she had trouble breathing.

She was having second thoughts. Apart from modesty, for Lena had always believed a respectable woman always kept her body covered, and she felt like a fraud.

Mabel gave her a good looking over when she'd finished.

"Do you think those men will believe I'm a Temperance lady?" Lena asked.

"Just pull a long face and act offended when they offer you a beer," Mabel replied.

"I don't suppose the men will notice the dress is a bit snug," she said.

"Lena," Mabel replied, as Lena turn away from the mirror, "those men won't be looking at the dress."

Mabel covered her mouth as she chortled. Lena didn't mind. Lord knows Mabel hadn't had a lot to laugh about in a long time.

"Why are you doing this?" Mabel handed her the black hat with the ruffled brim.

She tried it on. "Because it needs doing."

"Looks like the hat fits," Mabel said.

Lena lifted the skirt and tucked the pistol in the garter. It felt cold against her skin.

"I've never been brave," Mabel confessed.

Lena would hear such talk. "You crossed dried-up

plains, swollen rivers and a desert and lived to tell about it. That's courage enough for most folks."

Mabel grasped her hand.

Whether she knew it or not, Mabel had bolstered Lena's resolve with her easy friendship. "Thank you for your help."

Mabel gave her hand a squeeze and let her go. Lena picked up the leaflets.

"Don't forget to remind them of the evils of drink," Mabel said.

"Those boys won't listen," she told her. "Besides, where those boys are going, the evils of drink, so I've been told, will be the least of their worries."

Chapter Eight

THERE'D BEEN MANY a time when Lena Carlson had been afraid. Just as Mabel had done, Lena had walked across the Great Plains, forded treacherous rivers with reluctant oxen and buried the dead alongside the trail after a run of cholera or yellow fever swept through their wagon train.

Many times she was sure she would die as so many others had done. When the wagon train arrived in Ragtown, she believed it was nothing short of a miracle.

This fine fall day, standing in the streets of Virginia City, the cold fear of dying returned with a vengeance. What she was about to do was pure foolishness. Her practical nature reminded her that she was taking on more than any sensible person would.

What she'd do after she stepped inside the Gentleman's Drinking Club, she'd no idea. The gun was snug against her leg. Would she be able to use it?

Caroline Barrett would be afraid. What she'd been through would be a terrible ordeal for any woman. Those outlaws were drinking. Her life could be in considerable danger.

Lena tied the black silk ribbon of the heavy bonnet underneath her chin. She could scarcely breathe a lungful of air because of the corset. She'd started to perspire as the shimmering noonday sun soaked into the black fabric of

Mabel's dress.

She kicked out the flowing skirt. The starched petti-
coats crackled like paper. She'd never worn such finery.
Obviously, she wasn't cut out to be a society lady.

That didn't seem to matter to Henry. He'd kissed her
with a fair amount of interest and when this was over, she
meant to have him kiss her again. There was a lot of
potential in a man who could kiss as well as he'd done.

Lena grabbed a handful of her skirt and petticoat and
started down the boardwalk. She walked as quickly as
crushing whalebone would allow, a lady bent on destroy-
ing the demon rum.

Joseph stopped her as she crossed the street.

"Can't come this way, ma'am," he said.

She looked up into his young, lean face. He held an old
muzzle loader across his chest, meaning to protect the
citizens of Virginia City.

"I'm with the sheriff," she said.

"Sorry, ma'am but I have my orders. The sheriff
doesn't want anybody in the street while he makes an
arrest."

"I'm not just anybody," Lena said with growing confidence. "My name is Nicolena Carlson and I've come from
the Old Country. I'm a citizen of this territory and owner
of the Carlson Mercantile in Ragtown. I'll thank you to let
me pass."

The boy kept his stance. She could see he was depend-
able, a boy a mother could be proud of.

"I'm carrying a weapon," she said. "Do you want to
see where?"

Joseph went as red as his union suit.

She smiled with affection. "Don't you worry, Joseph.
I'll not shame you but I do intend to walk up this street.

Sheriff Maynard will not blame you."

Lena walked by him with her head up. He made no attempt to stop her. Strictly speaking, she'd violated Charlie's orders and he'd fault the boy for letting Lena through. Lena would make sure Charlie knew Joseph had done his job properly and bravely.

She continued down the middle of the empty street. An orange tomcat ran out from under the boardwalk. Startled, her hand flew to her chest. The tom continued on his way, more scared of her than she'd been of him.

When she reached the block of buildings where Henry, Charlie and his men waited out the gang, again she stopped. She'd no idea if Henry'd been successful rescuing Charlie from his hiding place behind the watering trough. She didn't dare look in that direction or at the other deputies positioned in the windows and behind the wagon. She didn't want to see Henry's angry face when he realized who it was dressed up in the black silk dress and bonnet. She wasn't about to let him stop her.

When she stepped up onto the boardwalk, a rifle's breech snapped shut. No one dared call out to her. It would be suicide if the men inside the saloon knew she was with the sheriff.

She hesitated, her heart thumping to the sound of the big rock crushers. She'd never in her life been inside a saloon. No lady who thought highly of her reputation would set foot in such a place. Her good sense told her the plan wouldn't work but a fierce protective nature, like a mother bear, pushed her forward.

If citizens didn't stand up to desperadoes, then lawlessness would prevail.

The batwing doors were pockmarked with bullet holes. One of them hung at an angle. She shoved the lopsided door aside and stepped into the murky light of a small room.

A man crouched beside each of the windows, his rifle ready. Another man eyed her with curiosity but didn't act like she concerned him at all. Sun streamed in through the broken glass, illuminating particles of dust floating lazily in the air. Sawdust coated the floor.

She took another step. Three men sat hunched over a square table playing cards. A woman wearing a fancy yellow dress and straw-colored hair piled up on her head watched, her arm around the neck of one of the men. A bartender, wearing a white linen shirt and sleeve-garters, gave Lena a sideways glance and then continued filling three glasses with a dark brown liquid.

A pretty girl sat at a table by herself, her hands folded in her lap. She was dressed in a traveling suit and wore a jaunty hat perched on her head. She looked more composed than a girl in her situation should be. In fact, if Lena were to guess her mood, she'd say the girl looked bored.

Lena was thankful no harm had come to Caroline Barrett and she gave her a reassuring smile. The girl didn't smile back. She looked casually at Lena and returned her gaze to the man playing cards with the saloon woman draped on his neck.

Lena understood that gaze and its significance frightened her.

A match flared and the man lit a cigarette. He looked up at Lena. A red glow illuminated his face. He was uncommonly handsome with the fair hair and the vivid blue eyes of the old country. He wore a woolsey shirt and a red bandana around his neck.

He shook out the match and threw it on the floor. "What do you want?"

Lena guessed he was the leader of the gang. She couldn't help but wonder how he'd started this life of crime. How killing became a way of life.

"My name is Lena Carlson. I've come to talk to you about the evils of drink."

Every pair of eyes turned their way when Lena spoke. The desperado sat back in his chair and blew out a mouthful of smoke. A rumble started from deep in this gullet, a menacing sound. He slapped his knee and burst into raucous laughter. The others joined him.

The saloon lady laughed the loudest. She was drunk and stumbled backward. The man pulled her into his lap and she squealed.

The outlaw looked pleased with himself and squeezed her on the mound of white bosom that showed above her fancy dress. The saloon lady didn't seem to mind at all and kissed him on the neck.

Caroline Barrett stiffened.

The outlaw picked up a silver coin from his winnings on the table and tossed it at Lena. The coin clinked on the floor and rolled to the foot of the bar.

"Why don't you bend over and pick that up?" the outlaw said.

The other men agreed that it would be a fine sight to see the Temperance Union lady in such a position. The men stationed at the front windows taunted her with more bawdy talk. They weren't paying attention to the street and Lena could only pray that Henry and the others would take advantage of their carelessness.

Lena drew herself taller as the men grew friskier. She'd never been around men with such poor manners and low regard for womenfolk. The gang thought she was as harmless as a newborn. A mistake they'd regret.

The pistol would take several seconds to remove from the garter. She would have to bide her time until an opportunity presented itself.

A six-shooter lay on the table next to the gang leader's stack of silver dollars. If she could get his gun, she would hold it on him until Henry arrived.

Her gaze lifted to the outlaw's face. He smiled broadly at her. Had he seen her look at the weapon? Had he guessed her purpose?

"I've brought some pamphlets," she said diligently. "If you'd only take a moment to read one. I'm sure you'll agree..."

"Barkeep. Whiskey."

The jeers grew louder. The outlaw pushed the saloon woman off his lap and sat up in his chair. He gestured at the bartender to bring over more drinks.

The bartender set two glasses on a metal tray. "Bring the bottle," the outlaw said.

The bartender did as he was told. He carried the tray with the bottle and placed it in front of the outlaw.

The outlaw poured the whiskey into the glass, right to the brim. "Now show the lady to the door."

Lena knew the time had come. She wouldn't have another chance to grab his weapon once the bartender put his hands on her.

She marched over to their table. "You look like an intelligent man." She set a pamphlet on the table in front of him.

His blue-eyed gaze mocked her. He picked up his glass and tossed the spirits at her.

The liquid hit her in the neck and trickled down the bodice of Mabel's dress. Lena gasped and wiped the burning spirits away with her hand. He laughed and looked around the room. The others laughed with him.

Lena seized her chance. She reached over and pounced on his gun. It was surprisingly heavy. She dropped the remaining leaflets on the ground and gripped the weapon with both hands.

"Put your hands in the air," she said, stepping away from the table.

"Now hold on, little lady," the outlaw said, smirking.

She pulled back the hammer and aimed at his forehead. He raised his hands slowly.

"Tell your men to set their rifles on the ground." Lena held the gun steadily on the man at the table. The outlaw quit smirking.

"I guess we have to do what she says, boys. Let the lady give her speech."

The men set their guns on the floor of the saloon. No one was laughing.

"Put up your hands. All of you." Her voice shook.

They raised their hands reluctantly.

Lena glanced at the bartender. He didn't take her meaning or chose to ignore what she needed him to do. Instead he hurried back behind the bar. Lena despaired, but she'd no time to explain. She turned briefly to Caroline. The girl seemed frozen to her chair.

Her hands cramped but she didn't dare move a muscle. She knew she was outmatched. "If any one of your men makes a move in my direction, I'll kill you," she said. "By God I will."

She depended on his believing her. His hands remained in the air.

"Now you get up and move toward the door," she said with more composure than she should have.

"Let's not be hasty," he said with boyish charm. "Me

and the boys were only having a bit of fun."

"I will shoot if you don't move and fast."

His expression turned dark and dangerous. She'd called his bluff in a game that could be deadly.

He stood, knocking over his chair. She kicked the chair aside, her aim never leaving the outlaw's head, her finger on the trigger.

"Lena, are you all right?"

She turned to see Henry Barrett barging through the swinging door with the Sharps at the ready. The broken hinge came out and the door crashed to the ground.

One of the outlaws tripped him before Lena could call out a warning. The rifle dropped to the floor as Henry fell forward.

She was grabbed from behind and her arms bent behind her. The gun tumbled out of her hand and onto the floor. The outlaw leader put his snout in her ear. Foul breath tightened her innards.

"Now you interfering old busybody, you're going to do what I say." He spoke in a raspy voice, a sound choked with hatred.

Henry sat up, holding his injured head.

"Leave her be," he said.

The outlaw picked up his gun and held it on Henry. "Shut up, or you're going to be the first to die."

"What are you doing?" Caroline asked in a shrill voice. She stood and stomped her foot.

"What do you care?" the outlaw asked.

"This man is my father," she said.

"Well, then, sweetheart, I mean to kill your old man."

Lena shivered. For sure, he'd the devil in him.

Caroline's eyes grew wider. "Whatever for?"

"Because I can."

"Let's just leave," Caroline said reasonably. "He's hurt. He won't follow us."

"You're right. He won't follow us." Her captor tightened his painful grip on Lena. "Not after I'm through with him."

Lena knew that struggling would get her nowhere. The outlaw was too strong. She did what ladies in trying circumstances are expected to do. She tilted her head to one side and wilted.

The outlaw's grip broke as she collapsed to the ground.

"Now, that's more like it," the outlaw said. He held his gun steady on Henry.

Lena pulled herself up by the brass railing of the bar, already forgotten.

Caroline, to her credit, stepped between her father and the man who held Henry's life in his hands.

"I won't let you shoot my father," she said with more haughtiness than was necessary to get her point across.

The outlaw slapped Caroline across the face with the back of his hand.

The girl tumbled to the ground, knocking over a lamp. Sawdust caught fire and an acrid smoke filled the room.

Henry sprung to his feet and grabbed the outlaw's gun hand. The outlaw clawed at Henry's face but Henry hung on. Lena lifted her skirt and pulled the pistol out of the garter. She held the gun on the pair fighting.

"That's enough," she said, coughing.

The outlaw looked at her, wild-eyed and desperate. His hands were around Henry's throat. The barkeep had finally found his courage and brought out a shotgun from behind the bar. He aimed it at the rest of the gang. Those boys didn't hesitate putting their hands in the air.

"I have one shot and I know where to put it," she said,

trying to keep her voice steady.

Henry landed an elbow just beneath the man's jaw. He yelped and let Henry go.

She tossed Henry her weapon. The outlaw raised his six-shot and fired.

Henry dropped and pulled off a single shot, hitting the outlaw between the eyes.

The suddenness of the shooting or the corset, Lena couldn't be sure, made her gasp. Caroline screamed. At the sound of gunfire, Charlie and his men stormed the saloon.

Lena looked anxiously at Henry. He sat up holding his shoulder but thankfully, she didn't see any blood. The bullet had missed him. He rose to his feet with difficulty, coughing as smoke swirled around them. He leaned over the outlaw and took the gun from his hand. He swung around and turned the weapon on the rest of the gang while the bartender poured water on the fire that danced across the floor.

"Tie 'em up," Henry said to the sheriff's men. "If any of you men tries anything, you'll end up joining your friend here in an early grave."

As the deputies took rope from the outlaws' gear and hogtied the men, Lena went to comfort Caroline who curled up on the floor next to the body of the outlaw and wept.

Lena looked over at Henry who scowled. Caroline had fallen for the wrong kind of man. A girl's mistake. Whether her father would be able to forgive her wasn't up to Lena.

"There, there," Lena said tenderly.

She found contentment in comforting the girl. Tears of her own threatened to break through but she held back. Caroline needed her strength and she'd cry tears of joy and thankfulness later.

Caroline sniffed and shuddered but stopped her crying.

"My heart is broken," she told Lena.

"I know."

"What will I do now?"

"You'll have to speak to the sheriff."

Caroline Barrett had no idea the trouble she'd gotten into. The girl would pay a heavy price for her foolishness if the sheriff saw fit to charge her.

"Hello, Caroline," Henry said, standing over them. His voice rumbled like distant thunder. His eyes were coals of burning male fury.

The girl stood and faced her father. She looked like she was about to eat him alive.

"Why did you have to kill him?" she asked.

"He deserved to die."

"He was the only man I ever loved."

"You didn't love him," Henry replied.

Caroline's lower lip trembled. "It would be difficult for you to recognize such a thing as love."

Henry didn't flinch but his nostrils flared.

Those two are so alike, Lena reckoned, as stubborn as mules and difficult about finding a spot in their hearts for forgiveness.

Caroline glared pure hatred at her father and then hurried out of the room.

"Go after her," Lena said.

"No, she's angry at me and there's nothing I could say to shift her."

"She's terribly hurt."

"I expect so."

She reached out to soothe his anger and hurt. He pulled away.

"What did you think you were doing?" He'd turned red and was breathing fire.

"Saving your girl," she reminded him.

"You could've been killed."

"I wasn't."

Henry didn't see fit to congratulate her. Without another word, he strode out the door.

Lena was in her own kind of temper. She'd expected thanks from Henry or at the least recognition for her part in capturing the gang and rescuing his daughter.

He'd withdrawn again into his shell. Plainly, he wanted to be miserable.

She couldn't bear that he would turn away from her, that her love wouldn't be enough.

Chapter Nine

HENRY DIDN'T WANT to stay in Virginia City for the night and Lena agreed. The sooner they set out for Ragtown, the sooner she'd be sleeping in her own comfortable featherbed. They replenished their supplies and said their good byes.

The surviving outlaws were left in the capable hands of Charlie Maynard. They would be waiting for justice in the form of a hangman's noose. The men's horses were given to the barkeep to pay for the damages to the saloon.

Charlie hadn't held charges against Caroline Barrett, explaining how she hadn't been carrying a weapon and how he'd come across this kind of case before. He knew a girl held captive could be easily swayed by a rough-riding kind of man.

Henry wouldn't accept payment for what he'd done and they left with a promise they'd be back soon for a real visit.

Caroline rode behind Lena.

Lena saw a willingness to know Caroline better in Charlie's gaze and manner but Caroline primly ignored him. The girl was willful and headstrong, Lena decided, and she'd a lot to learn about the differences between good men and those who would hurt her.

She turned and looked at Caroline. There was never a sorrier sight than that girl in her dirty and torn traveling dress and lopsided hat. She clutched a lacy handkerchief and dabbed at her eyes.

Lena straightened in her seat. Tears would do the girl no good. She'd have to call on that strong will of hers to survive in this hostile land.

As soon as the town was behind them, Henry turned sullen. He was sore at Lena for dressing up like she'd done and going into the saloon. Plainly, he didn't know how to deal with an unhappy daughter.

Forgiveness just wasn't in his nature, Lena realized. Forgiving himself was out of the question.

Henry was still determined about putting her on the stage heading east and Caroline could only pine after a man who'd been the worst kind of man for her to love.

Never had Lena been so disgusted with a pair. Father and daughter had a chance to be a family but neither would budge an inch from their opinions. Lena was at a loss on how to bring them together.

The blue sky began to deepen and the wind blew colder. The three of them were worn through and soon they'd need to stop for the night. There would be awkwardness with those two not talking to each other, Lena reckoned, and the evening would be an uncomfortable one.

THEY CAMPED IN the shelter of some rocks. Others had camped here before, maybe even Henry although he didn't say as he took care of the horses.

Lena pushed blackened rocks together to make a better circle. This was a good place for a warm fire, away from the wind. She brushed off her hands and straightened.

"We'd better gather up some firewood," she said to

Caroline. The girl plopped down on a nearby boulder and sighed.

Lena allowed that Caroline had no experience living outdoors but her attitude needed correcting.

"I need your help to get a fire going."

The girl looked at her. In the growing darkness Lena could barely see her face.

"Let him do it," Caroline said, nodding in the direction of her papa.

"Your papa has his chores," Lena said. "If we don't have a fire, we'll be eating jerky and crackers this night."

Caroline stood. Clearly, she didn't like that she'd no say in the matter but she started picking up brush. Lena watched her with growing affection.

"Why does my father have to be so mean?" Caroline asked as they walked together each carrying an armload.

"There's no meanness in him but he's tough. He remembers how your mama died. He doesn't want you to face the same hardship."

"I won't go back to St. Joseph. Please, Lena, persuade him to let me stay."

"You'll have to do the persuading."

"He won't listen."

"Then show him."

They built a good fire. Coffee heated on a flat rock next to the flames and bacon fried in an iron pan. Lena mixed cornmeal, soda and water and poured the mixture over the crackling bacon. They hadn't eaten since morning and the smells aroused her hunger.

Henry sat down without speaking. Caroline rose from her seat and poured coffee into a tin cup. She handed it to her papa.

Lena smiled. She'd done what she could. Whether these

two could ever mend their differences was up to them. She looked for a crack in Henry's stern demeanor, some awareness that the girl was trying but he didn't say more than a handful of words during the entire meal. When she'd banked the fire and they'd turned in for the night, Henry settled down in his bedroll and slept with his back to them.

THE FIRST HINT that they were close to Ragtown was the pair of fish eagles that flew overhead. Their horses picked up the pace, smelling water from the Carson River.

They'd been riding since dawn and as they arrived in the town, the rays of a late day sun beat down on them. Who was there to greet them but that old yellow dog. He stood on the boardwalk barking a greeting and Lena was glad to see him.

They rode down the street. Curious passers-by shrank back and whispered behind their hands. Mr. Belknap came out of the barbershop holding a straight razor. Soon it seemed like the entire town gawked at them from a safe distance, of course.

Lena stayed back and let Henry take the lead.

Henry dismounted in front of the Mercantile. "Gents," he said to the men gathered there.

Big Jim pushed in front of them. "Did you get them?"

"The leader died in a shootout," Henry told them. "The rest are with the Virginia City sheriff and will stand trial."

Lena slid down to the ground. She'd never been so sore. Her body ached in every direction. She was glad to be home.

The men, eager for more news, pressed closer. She thought she'd be angry with them for not forming a posse and following Henry and her to the Comstock. She wasn't. They all were brave men and wouldn't shy away from defending their homes but they weren't gun fighters any more than Henry was a placer miner.

"I'll take care of the horses," Big Jim said.

"Thank you," she said and favored him with a weary smile.

Henry turned to his daughter. "Ragtown is no place for you. You'll take a room at the hotel and wait on the next stage coming through."

"Why don't you want me here?" The girl's pride had been wounded and she lashed out at her papa.

Henry's face creased. "You wouldn't last long in this rugged land."

"I want to stay."

Henry rested his hand on his hips and shifted his weight. "The territory isn't a place for a lady."

"I can stay with Lena. Tell him, Lena, that I can stay with you." Caroline's gaze pleaded with Lena to give her a home.

Lena warmed to the idea and she'd like nothing better but this was a matter between them. "I'd be pleased to have you stay with me but you need to convince your papa."

Henry looked at Lena with gratitude. He hadn't been sure of her support. It troubled Lena that Henry would doubt her.

He turned back to Caroline. "I've made up my mind. You're going."

Caroline wanted the last word. She glared at Henry. "Don't think you can tell me what to do."

Lena opened her mouth to say something to keep the two from hurting each other with caustic words but maybe it was better for them to air their differences.

She left the Barretts arguing on the boardwalk.

THE TINY BELL on the Mercantile door rang steadily all afternoon. Everybody in the territory seemed to come to town and found they needed supplies. They emptied the shelves and nobody haggled, not even Mr. Andresen, who could drive a hard bargain. Their goodwill poured into the dry goods store like a healing salve.

Lena received heartfelt embraces from the women and men removed their hats when they came through the door. She regarded them all with affection, for she knew they tried to thank her in the best way they knew how for going after Henry and that ruthless gang.

They plied her with questions about the outlaws and how they'd met their fate.

Most gasped in horror and disbelief when she told them what they'd done.

Lena had moments of disbelief herself when she described her adventure as a Temperance Union lady. What possessed her to defy Henry and take on that bloodthirsty gang, she'd probably never know. The gang's lawless ways were done and Caroline had been saved and everyone in town congratulated Lena on her courage.

When the last sale had been rung up and the final customer walked out the door, Lena closed her store. Her body sagged with fatigue but she needed to find Henry. He was wrong about Caroline and she hoped he'd come to the same conclusion she had.

The man was obstinate and not easily persuaded. She'd been sincere about letting Caroline make her own case for staying. Lena had something important to tell him. All of the residents of Ragtown's good wishes and ready cash didn't mean as much to her as Henry's affections.

She removed her apron and put on a clean bonnet. She didn't bother to lock the door behind her.

Nobody'd seen which way Henry and his girl had gone. Lena knew Henry didn't have any money and wouldn't ask for credit. With growing trepidation, she headed for the livery.

Lazarus carried a pail of water from the town trough.

"Have you seen Henry?" she asked.

Lazarus poured the water into a barrel. "As soon as he'd put some victuals together, he hightailed out of town on that mule he thinks so of highly of."

Lena felt hollow inside. "What about his daughter?"

"She wasn't with him."

She thanked Lazarus and hurried away. Henry's departure without saying goodbye after all they'd experienced and shared crushed her. Even though she suspected he wanted to heal up and not be troubled by any more questions, his leaving so soon was a heavy blow.

Lena went to the hotel, the only place a respectable girl could stay. She rousted Mr. Andresen from his supper.

"Is Miss Caroline Barrett staying here?" she asked.

He pulled off his kerchief and wiped his mouth. "She came in this afternoon. She's staying until the next stage pulls through."

"I'd like to see her."

"Be my guest. The girl hasn't left her room since she arrived and refused the meal that came with her lodging."

Mr. Andresen told her which room Caroline had taken.

Lena climbed the stairs and knocked on the door.

"Caroline, it's me, Lena. Can I speak with you?"

"Go away," Caroline replied behind the door.

"Please Caroline, we should talk."

"I have nothing to say to you."

She was too angry at the world, Lena suspected, to take solace from a friend. She'd try again tomorrow, for Lena had a stubborn streak of her own when it came to helping those she cared about.

As for Henry Barrett, she wished things had turned out differently but wishing wouldn't change him. He was obstinate to a fault. He'd a fixed estimation of every subject and didn't budge from an opinion. Lena'd thought they made a good team but she was wrong. Henry preferred a solitary life.

Lena could only shake her head and exclaim to Mr. Andresen how she'd never met such a stubborn pair as the Barretts.

He asked her if she'd eaten.

"No," she said sighed.

"There's plenty and room for you any day at our table," the man said.

Lena didn't feel like conversation. Her hurt was too deep to talk yet about it. She thanked the innkeeper, deeply touched by his offer.

If he guessed her trouble, he didn't let on.

She walked back to the Mercantile. The sun was setting. The days were getting shorter and frost nipped in the evening air.

Folks hurried to finish their chores and head home to their suppers. Hunger gnawed at her but what felt worse was the finality of Henry's actions. She needed to put him out of her mind and go home and make her own supper.

First she had business at the bank.

LENA EMPTIED THE cash register and counted the silver and
gold coins and the paper bills. The day's take had been
good. She put the money into a leather bag to deposit in
her account. Luckily, Mr. Kemp kept late hours so the
businesses in town could put their receipts in the bank's
vault at the end of every day. By anyone's measure, he was
a valued businessman with a concern for the security of the
town's money.

She didn't look forward to meeting with him but she
couldn't avoid him for the rest of her years. She'd come to
a decision and even though she had another day to give
him her answer, she wanted to face the man now and be
over and done with it.

"Come sit down," Mr. Kemp said, rubbing his hands
together. He indicated the minuscule chair across from his
big oak desk. "I'm glad you're back from the Comstock in
one piece."

Lena sank down and took a deep breath. Her trip to
Virginia City had been an adventure beyond her wildest
imaginings and she'd never forget it.

Mr. Kemp seated himself opposite. His face brightened
at the bag of money she placed on his desk.

"The Mercantile is doing well," he said. He pulled a
ledger out of the desk drawer and licked his fingers as he
turned the large pages.

"My best day ever," she agreed. She didn't tell him
how the store had been filled to capacity all afternoon and
how the residents had bought things they didn't even need.
She doubted a man such as Mr. Kemp would understand

why.

"Let's see. Yes, here we are. The Carlson Mercantile, soon, I hope, to be the Kemp Mercantile." His face glowed, like a child with a new toy, in anticipation of her acceptance of his proposal.

She waited as he counted out the silver coins and then the gold. Finally, he counted the stack of paper currency. After he recorded her deposit and handed her a receipt, Lena was ready to speak her mind.

"Mr. Kemp, I'll get straight to the point. I appreciate the offer of marriage." The banker closed the ledger and folded his hands on top.

"I can't marry you."

His amiable demeanor evaporated. He returned to his businessman self. "I don't understand. I thought we had an agreement."

"Mr. Kemp, it seems to me you don't need my dry goods store and you don't need any more wealth. What you need is a wife who loves you and a herd of strong children to call your own."

His face turned the color of her shawl. "But surely, Mrs. Carlson..."

"I don't love you and I can't give you sons to carry on your name and daughters to take care of you when you grow too old to run the bank."

Mr. Kemp sat back in his chair. "You're making a grave mistake," he managed to say after what she'd said soaked in.

"That may be," Lena was willing to admit. "All my born days, I haven't felt this strongly about a subject."

"You can't expect to run that store without the guidance of a husband," he said, repeating what he'd told her at the beginning of the week.

"I intend to do just that." She drew herself to her full height and looked him straight in the eye. "You're right about growing the town and I expect more families will settle here as the territory becomes more peaceful. I will help you and the other good citizens of Ragtown the best I know how. We can help each other."

She stood. She'd said what she'd come to say.

Mr. Kemp stayed put. "You'll regret this."

Of course, the banker hadn't expected her to turn him down. He intended to have her store one way or the other. They'd be adversaries instead of friends, a sad commentary on his character but not hopefully on the future of their town.

She pocketed her receipt. "Good day, Mr. Kemp," she said with unashamed confidence. She turned and walked out of the room.

THE VERY NEXT morning, as Lena packed a box with supplies for the Campaniles, she looked up to see the one face that always sent her heart fluttering. Henry came walking through the door of the Mercantile. He'd trimmed his beard and put on a clean shirt under his buckskin jacket. He wore a new short-brimmed hat.

To Lena's way of thinking, he looked like a piece of heaven.

"Now, Lena, don't you forget that box of buckshot," Mrs. Campanile said.

Lena added a box to the woman's basket.

As Henry approached them, Mrs. O'Malley clutched her parcel like a shield. Two women examining a bolt of calico nudged each other.

"It's good to see you, Henry," Lena said, cordially. She saw no reason to be unfriendly. "How's your shoulder?"

"The shoulder's tolerable."

"I see the gash in your head is healing."

"Yes, Ma'am. Thanks to your good care."

Lena fought a blush. "You're a day early. The stage doesn't come through until tomorrow."

"I missed your chatter," he replied. "It was too quiet out there on my claim."

Lena put her hand on her bosom, willing the thunderous beating to stay quiet. "Why Henry Barrett. What are you saying?"

He rubbed his face. She caught a whiff of the sweet-smelling shaving lotion Mr. Belknap used over at the barbershop.

"I missed you." He wasn't a man to waste words.

Lena didn't reply to what he'd said. They'd unfinished business to settle before she could let him claim her heart.

"What about Caroline? She wants to stay and live in Ragtown."

"I've made up my mind about her," he said. "She's going back to St. Jo where she belongs."

"Why are you so set on her leaving?"

"We've talked this all through before." He was clearly exasperated with her pressing the matter but she wouldn't give up.

"Have you asked her what she wants?"

"You know she's not talking to me."

"Don't you know why?" Lena sighed. The ways of women were still foreign to him. "Now you listen to me. You have a daughter who thinks you don't love her."

Henry's eyes widened. "That ain't so."

"No matter. She thinks that way and you need to correct that notion."

He shook his head. "She's a different breed of female. I can't risk her staying. You seen her, Lena. She's like her ma. This land will kill her surely as it did her ma."

Lena had to admit the girl did have a lot to learn about living in the territory. "She needs you no matter what kind of person she is or isn't."

Henry scowled.

"From what I've seen, there's a lot of you in her."

His scowled softened. "I reckon there is a bit of wildcat in that girl."

Lena put her hand on his arm. She wanted him to listen and listen good. "You can't protect the ones you love by keeping them at a distance."

Henry frowned.

Lena squeezed his arm and let him go. It would be difficult for him to admit he'd been wrong. She and the ladies of Ragtown watched him walk away, steady in his step, his big shoulders square and his back straight.

"You told him," Mrs. O'Malley said.

"He's heading for the hotel," Grandma Elias said as she spied at the window.

"He's going to see his girl," Mrs. O'Malley said in her squeaky voice.

Lena returned to her duties. She hadn't thought it possible that she could have such strong feelings for a man. Whatever happened, she'd told him the truth as she saw it.

More importantly, she'd spoken from the heart.

Whether he'd listened and would correct the error in his ways was up to him to decide.

Chapter Ten

A FEW HOURS later, Lena had her answer. Henry and Caroline strode across the road toward the Mercantile. Lena hurriedly finished with her customer and asked the lingering cowboys if they wouldn't mind returning on the morrow. She handed them a silver dollar each and told them to have a sarsaparilla with her compliments at the Easy saloon just down the block.

The cowboys were much obliged and Lena corralled them out of the store and turned over the Closed sign.

If there was going to be a confrontation, it wouldn't be in front of neighbors and friends. Or strangers, for that matter.

She needn't have worried. Henry was smiling. He looked so handsome when he did so. She met them at the door.

"Caroline and I wondered if you were free for supper," Henry said.

Lena checked with Caroline. She looked agreeable enough. "Supper?"

"Unless you've made other plans," he said.

"No. I expect supper cooked by somebody else would be just fine."

"We've got some talking to do," he said.

"If it's about what happened in Virginia City," she said. "I'm not sorry and I have no regrets."

"No. I expect you thought what you done was the best thing. I'm too mule-headed to appreciate it. That's behind us. We need to talk about the future."

"You know I can talk your arm off if need be."

He turned to Caroline. She gazed at her papa with admiration.

"My daughter tells me I have some hard edges," he said.

The girl's love of her papa spilled over into tears. Lena handed her a clean handkerchief. She dabbed at her eyes but her gaze never left her papa's face.

"We've a lot to sort out, my daughter and me. I need your help."

This turn of events had been everything Lena had hoped for but her practical nature cautioned her to be wary.

"All right, if this is what you want." Lena wrapped her shawl tighter.

A group of men approached them. They'd put on their Sunday best in the middle of the week. For what reason, Lena wouldn't even venture a guess.

"We've come to offer you a job," Big Jim said to Henry.

"What kind of job?"

"This town needs a sheriff," Mr. Belknap said. "We've been needing a good man to protect us from stage robbers and such like."

What Mr. Belknap said was only partly right but Lena didn't correct him. They believed it was a man's job to defend home and hearth but Lena knew better. A woman could do the job just as well.

"I don't rightly know," Henry replied. "I'd have to check with the womenfolk."

Lena crossed her arms and gave each of the town fathers a stern look. "What kind of wages is the town paying?"

The men looked at each other.

"We were thinking fifty dollars a month," Mr. Woodruff said.

Lena narrowed her eyes.

"Sixty, then."

"And traveling expenses," Lena said.

"As need be," Mr. Andresen replied.

"That sound good to you?" Lena asked Henry.

"Sounds like I could support a family on those wages," Henry said. He stuck out his hand. "We've got a deal."

The men shook hands vigorously as the ladies watched.

Big Jim took a tin badge out of his vest pocket and handed it over.

Henry pinned it on his shirt, looking pleased. He offered his arm to Lena and she clamped her hand around it. He offered his other arm to Caroline. She smiled shyly before accepting.

Excusing themselves from present company, they walked arm in arm down the boardwalk.

"I'll never be a wealthy man," Henry said.

"He sold his black mule to pay my hotel bill," Caroline said.

"Now Caroline, I told you not to carry on about that mule." Henry didn't speak sternly. Something had changed inside him.

"I'm sorry about the mule," Lena said sincerely.

"Lazarus gave me a good price. Seems he's taken a shine to the old boy." Henry smiled. "Now that I'm settling down, I won't be needing a mule anymore anyways."

"What are you saying, Mr. Barrett?"

"Seems to me what I need is a wife." His smile widened. "Are you willing?"

The man was clumsy with his words but he got his point across. She realized she'd been waiting for Henry her entire life. "I'm more than willing."

He kissed her lightly on the cheek. The sensation of pure joy ran down to her toes.

Caroline kissed her on the other cheek. "Now I have a mother and father," she said happily.

Lena kissed the girl's forehead. She'd never expected to have a daughter and now she would, thanks to Henry Barrett.

The three of them linked arms and continued down the boardwalk.

NOTICE IN THE New Year's edition of the *Territorial Enterprise*:

> *Sheriff Henry Barrett united in matrimony with Mrs. Nicolena Carlson December 29, 1861. The couple commenced housekeeping in Ragtown and are the proprietors of the Yellow Dog Mercantile.*

Dear Readers,

Come take a journey with me to Edwardian England and the American West where feisty heroines and the men they love find adventure and their happily ever after.

I write romance and strive to infuse each character with the personal courage and commitment to take the journey of self-discovery that will make them worthy to love. How my characters arrive at their destinations continues to amaze me.

My background is as American as apple pie. I was born and raised in northern Michigan, graduated from the University of Michigan, and worked as a Peace Corps Volunteer in Kenya.

Today my husband and I live in San Diego, the place of my heart, close to our beautiful children and grandchild.

I welcome your comments and I hope you'll join me on social media. Let me know what you are reading and what kinds of books you like.

With thanks,
Sarah

Facebook: facebook.com/sarahrichmondwriter
Twitter: twitter.com/srichmondwriter
Goodreads:
goodreads.com/author/show/1725233.Sarah_Richmond

Books about the American West by Sarah Richmond

Dulcie Crowder Gets Her Man

Brides of Serendipity
Courtin' Dory
Barrett's Law
Rosy
Angels with Dirty Faces

Also by Sarah Richmond

Rose Adagio
Past Forgetting
A Most Ineligible Suitor
Do Be Sensible, Miss Wynchcomb
A Perilous Proposal: Book One in the House of Caruthers
series
A Secret Engagement: Book Two in the House of
Caruthers series
A Wayward Wedding: Book Three in the House of
Caruthers series
Running on Empty
Mrs. Pratt's War

Find out more at **www.SarahRichmond.com**